WHAT WAS SHE DOING HERE?

What was Tracy doing in this huge mansion whose rooms she could not count and whose hallways were a bewildering maze?

What was she doing surrounded by servants who seemed determined not to let her lift a finger whether she wanted to or not?

What was she doing in the company of lords and ladies whose venomous gossip and razor-edged wit might well have been in a foreign tongue for all she could join in with them?

Above all, what was she doing as wife to the devilishly handsome and charming Duke who now waited for her in her bridal chamber?

Clearly, Adrian, the Duke of Hastings, had a great deal to teach Tracy about being a Duchess—and even more to learn if he didn't want a new American Revolution on his hands.

A

SIGNET Regency Romances You'll Enjoy

The
American Duchess

by
Joan Wolf

A SIGNET BOOK

NEW AMERICAN LIBRARY

TIMES MIRROR

Copyright © 1982 by Joan Wolf

All rights reserved

 SIGNET TRADEMARK REG. U.S. PAT. OFF. AND FOREIGN COUNTRIES
REGISTERED TRADEMARK—MARCA REGISTRADA
HECHO EN CHICAGO, U.S.A.

SIGNET, SIGNET CLASSICS, MENTOR, PLUME, MERIDIAN AND NAL
Books are published by The New American Library, Inc.,
1633 Broadway, New York, New York 10019

First Printing, December, 1982

1 2 3 4 5 6 7 8 9

PRINTED IN THE UNITED STATES OF AMERICA

Chapter 1

I have a daughter.
—Shakespeare

They went up the long staircase, wafted along by footmen, and at the top were met by a white-wigged major domo who took their names and announced in clear, measured tones, "The American Minister, Mr. Rush. Mr. Bodmin. Miss Bodmin."

The elegant, haughty-looking woman who stood on the wide landing receiving her guests smiled fractionally, her shrewd eyes taking careful measure of the newcomers. Richard Rush she knew. She was Lady Bridgewater and her husband, the Earl of Bridgewater, was a member of Lord Liverpool's government. This was a political reception she was hostessing and most of the diplomatic community had been invited.

The Bodmins were not from the diplomatic community. When Richard Rush had written to ask if he might bring them, he had given only a sketchy background of his visitors; but Lady Bridgewater had done some checking of her own. She looked

1

now, appraisingly, at the tall, wide-shouldered man whom she had been told was the greatest individual shipowner in the United States and the wealthiest man in New England. William Bodmin looked to be in his middle fifties. He had thick gray hair and thick straight eyebrows, a strongly jutting nose and firm chin. His whole demeanor proclaimed the unmistakable authority of ability, experience and success. He smiled now at Lady Bridgewater. "It was very kind of you to allow us to come, my lady. I was anxious to show my daughter some London parties and Rush here said he would trespass upon your good nature and ask if he might bring us along."

"I am very pleased to extend a welcome to such a distinguished visitor from overseas," Lady Bridgewater answered temperately. "You must let me make you known to my husband." Then, having passed the men along, she turned her attention to the girl.

Teresa Bodmin looked fearlessly back and waited for Lady Bridgewater to speak first. "Are you enjoying London, Miss Bodmin?" that lady asked after she had taken in every aspect of the girl's appearance.

"I hardly know," came the reply. "We've only been here a week, you see. I expect I shall like it once I get my bearings a bit." Her voice was clear and cultured and assured. Lady Bridgewater nodded a little with satisfaction and expertly handed her along to the Earl.

William Bodmin was unabashedly pleased to be at Bridgewater House. He passed through the rooms, his daughter's arm in his, and expanded visibly as his gaze took in the brilliant company—the men in immaculate evening dress, the women lovely and elegant in their dresses that left their shoulders bare.

"We don't have anything like this back in Salem, do we, Tracy?" he asked his daughter.

"No, Papa," she responded obediently.

"Not in Boston, either. Or New York. Or Washington. When it comes to *real* elegance, the English have it all over us."

His daughter looked at him curiously but said nothing. A little later, when her father was talking to Lord Bridgewater, Richard Rush asked her, "Are you enjoying yourself, Miss Bodmin?"

She wrinkled her nose a little and looked at him with laughing eyes. "Would it be odiously ungrateful of me if I told you I wasn't?"

"Why ungrateful?"

"Oh, after you went to all that trouble to get us invited."

"It was no trouble." He looked a little concerned. "Is there something I can do?"

"It isn't you, Mr. Rush," she said, briefly laying her hand on his sleeve. "It is just that we are strangers here, Papa and I. We look all right. We seem to blend in with everyone else, but we don't, really."

At that, Lady Bridgewater came up to them. "You must allow me to introduce you to a few people, Miss Bodmin," she said with a smile that was less haughty than the one she had bestowed upon Tracy at the door.

"That would be very nice," Tracy responded politely, if unenthusiastically, and allowed herself to be led away by the Countess. William Bodmin, rejoining Mr. Rush, watched them cross the room.

"I am very obliged to you, Rush, for bringing us tonight," he said once again to his fellow countryman. "These are just the sort of people I want Tracy to get to know."

"Lady Bridgewater is very aristocratic," said Mr. Rush carefully. "I shouldn't expect too much out of the acquaintance if I were you, Mr. Bodmin. Americans are acceptable for political receptions, but she is far too particular to invite us to one of her purely social affairs. One has to have a pedigree that goes back at least three hundred years to hope to achieve that honor."

William Bodmin went on watching his daughter's graceful progress with satisfaction. "Ten million dollars is an excellent pedigree," he said serenely.

"Yes," said Mr. Rush after a pause. "Yes, I guess it is."

Mr. Bodmin's sanguine expectations appeared to be borne out when, toward the end of the evening, Lady Bridgewater took the trouble of singling him out for a private conversation. "Your daughter is a charming girl, Mr. Bodmin," she told him.

Tracy's father smiled with honest pleasure. "She is the dearest thing in the world to me," he said. "My fondest hope is to see her settled in the kind of setting I think she deserves."

"Ah?" said Lady Bridgewater, raising a thin eyebrow. "Such a young lady deserves a beautiful setting indeed."

"She will be able to afford one," said Mr. Bodmin. "I will be blunt with you, Lady Bridgewater. I want to see my girl married. For what else have I toiled and struggled for all these years, but to see her settled? To see her well married? I want the best article on the market for my girl and I've come to England to get it. I know the best can't be had for mere money, but I rather think money will do a great deal. Tracy will do the rest."

Lady Bridgewater was looking at him thoughtfully. "You are blunt indeed, Mr. Bodmin." She smiled and tapped him on the arm. "Bring Miss Bodmin to call on me tomorrow."

William Bodmin smiled back. "You are very kind," he said, and Lady Bridgewater nodded and moved on.

The Bodmins duly called at Bridgewater House the next day and the Countess subjected Tracy to a ruthless scrutiny which she did not make much effort to conceal. The result of the visit was an invitation by Lady Bridgewater to accompany her to a ball being given the following evening by the Countess of Kincaid.

The ball was what Lady Bridgewater called a sad crush. Present were about five hundred of the cream of London society. Lady Bridgewater graciously introduced Tracy to half a dozen young men and sat back to watch the results.

The results were interesting indeed. Word soon spread that the extremely pretty girl who had come in with Lady Bridgewater was an American. Further waves of information disclosed that the large man with her was her father and that he was a millionaire. "I understand that he made a fortune out of trading with Russia during the war," said Lady Jersey to Mrs. Drummond Burrell. Lady Jersey had been talking to Lady Bridgewater.

"Yes, but how does Georgina know him?"

"I'm not sure, but Bridgewater is President of the Board of Trade, remember. It must be something to do with politics."

"Well, money is all very well, but who are they? One never knows with Americans."

"True. The girl is lovely, though." Here both aristocratic ladies paused to gaze critically at Miss Teresa Bodmin. The young man dancing with her was gazing as well, but not at all critically.

Tracy was worth looking at. She was tall and slender with a quantity of brown-blonde hair that fell in curls to her shoulders. If her father projected an aura of power and authority, Tracy's chief characteristic was vitality. Her skin glowed with health, her hazel eyes were bright and clear, her flashing smile showed straight white teeth; over all, she had a lovely, golden, young look that was extraordinarily attractive.

"She seems to know how to behave," said Mrs. Drummond Burrell a little grudgingly.

"Yes. I wonder what Georgina can have in mind," replied Lady Jersey, one of the patronesses of Almacks and guardians of the purity of English society.

William Bodmin watched his daughter and felt himself to be a happy man. This scheme of his of introducing Tracy to English society had been in the back of his mind for some time, and several events had recently occurred to cause him to finally put it into practice.

For one thing, Tracy had turned eighteen, and it was high time she married. He had also realized that if he didn't introduce her to an appropriate English young man shortly, she would undoubtedly attach herself to some American young man. There were several in Salem who showed every sign of attaching themselves to her—one Captain Adam Lancaster in particular. William Bodmin had a great liking and respect for Adam Lancaster, a young man who in many ways resembled him, but he wanted something else for Tracy.

Fifty-eight years ago William Bodmin had been born in a small fishing village in Cornwall. His only future had been the Royal Navy, which was nothing more than a living hell, so at age thirteen he had taken ship to America and landed in Salem. All through his early teens he had shipped as a boy on coasters; he had seen Demerara and Saint Petersburg before he ever set foot in Boston. By the time he was twenty-three he was in command of an East-Indiaman.

He had married Kathleen Breen, of Boston, whose father was a small shipowner. William Bodmin, however, was not destined for small things. By the time President Jefferson's embargo caught him in 1807, he was worth three million dollars.

New England was against the embargo, a self-blockade that confined American merchant ships to port. Its purpose was to demonstrate to the British that England must allow America, as a neutral power in the Napoleonic wars, to trade with Europe. The embargo hurt the English economy badly. Unfortunately, it also had a paralyzing effect on American commerce.

William Bodmin had supported the embargo. As a patriotic American he had said it was a necessary measure of self-protection. For his pains he had been expelled from the Federalist party, along with a fellow Massachusetts rebel, John Quincy Adams. Bodmin had sacrificed financial profit and social position by his stand, but he had stuck to it. And when the embargo was lifted, he had made more money.

Why, then, was this man—a truly patriotic American, who had personally financed the outfitting of two naval ships during the late war against England and who was fiercely proud of, and devoted to, his adopted country—so determined to marry his only child into the English aristocracy? The answer to that question went back many years to his boyhood in Cornwall, when he had observed with awe and wonder the lords and ladies of the "Great House" in his neighborhood. He had thought then that no way of life could ever rival that of the English aristocracy, and nothing he had seen since then had caused him to change his mind. It was not the life for him; he did not aspire to it and would not know what to do with it if he ever came into it, but it was the life he wanted for his girl.

So now he looked around the glittering ballroom and smiled with contentment. So firmly convinced was he of the superiority of what he was viewing that it never occurred to him to wonder if his daughter might think differently.

Chapter 2

His greatness weighed, his will is not his own,
For he himself is subject to his birth.
                                        —Shakespeare

"Dash it all, Mary, you're not paying attention!" The speaker was Lord Harry Deincourt and the person he was addressing so petulantly was his sister.

Lady Mary looked up from her book. "Harry, if you say one word more about the weather, I shall scream with vexation."

Lord Harry thrust out his underlip, sighed heavily and stared out the window at the unrelenting rain. He was fourteen years old and had been sent home from school for the rest of the term for pulling a prank that the authorities had not found amusing. He had just spent an extremely unpleasant fifteen minutes with his elder brother, the Duke of Hastings, and wanted to get outdoors on a horse to relieve his feelings. But it was raining.

Mary put down her book. "What did Adrian say?"

9

Harry sat down, stretched his legs out in front of him and looked unhappily at his fifteen-year-old sister. "I tell you what, Mary, I'd much rather have father ranting and swearing at me for hours at a time than spend fifteen minutes such as I spent this morning with Adrian. He never raises his voice, but he's got a way of making himself disagreeable when he wishes that is dashed unnerving."

"Well, you deserved it," his sister said unsympathetically. "Staying out all night to see some stupid prizefight! You are fortunate they are allowing you to come back next year."

"Mmph," said Harry, his lip more prominent than ever.

"Adrian has enough to worry about," Mary said with unusual gravity. "You should have enough sense not to add to it."

There was silence as Lord Harry scuffed his feet on the floor. "It's money, isn't it?" he brought out gruffly after a minute.

"Yes. I asked Adrian if we were in serious trouble and he said I was not to worry, that things would all come right. But I *do* worry." She frowned. "It was wicked of Papa, Harry, to gamble the way he did. Just look at the mess he has landed us in."

"If Adrian said it would all come right, it will," said Harry, who combined a healthy respect for his brother's tongue with an almost blind belief in his other abilities. A man, Harry reasoned, who had had three horses shot out from under him at Waterloo and had not got a scratch himself, a man like that could do anything. Putting the noble house of Hastings back on its financial feet would be child's play to such a man. He looked at the window and sighed. "If only it would stop raining."

Mary screamed.

The Duke of Hastings was, like his brother, gazing out at the rain and, like his brother, he had no doubts that he could find the means to put his house back in order. He had spent several months working with his man of business, and the picture he had been left with was not pleasant. Like Mary, he felt anger at his father. And at his grandfather as well, for the financial downfall of the Deincourt family had not been the work of only one generation. The Duke knew all too well the history of the doings and the follies of his ancestors, particularly of their infamous waste of money that should have come to him.

There had been nothing he could do to prevent his father from gambling. In the end, to avoid the inevitable rows that their proximity always gave rise to, the Duke had taken himself off. He had been the Earl of Hythe then, and as soon as he had come down from Oxford he had joined the army and gone out to the Peninsula. He had remained on the Continent until his father's death: in the Peninsula, at the Congress of Vienna, at Waterloo, and then with the Army of Occupation in Paris, serving as aide to the Duke of Wellington. When his father had died in October, he had sold out and come home.

He was the Duke of Hastings, one of the premier nobles in all of Great Britain. He bore a name which had resonated throughout all of English history. Pride in his heritage, in his race and in his name and position had come to him as part of his birthright. It was his duty to ensure that that name and that position were upheld in an appropriate manner. But that manner required money, and at present money was something he sorely lacked.

It had not taken the Duke long to decide upon his course of action. If he had no money, then his wife should. He felt little, if any, repugnance at the idea of marrying for money. He was the head of his family now, and it was necessary that he act, not for his own pleasure, but for the advantage of the family. Nor did he feel he would be doing an injustice to the lady, unspecified as yet, whom he planned to make his wife. She would be the Duchess of Hastings; that in itself would content many women. And he would be a satisfactory husband. It was a question, he thought, of doing the best for one's self that one could—without injury to others. He had little doubt as to his success. He had an implicit faith that whatever the outcome he might desire he would always absolutely bring it off.

He looked from the window back to the letter that lay on his table.

"My dear Adrian," it read. "I am giving a small reception Wednesday next week and I should like you to attend. There is a young lady I particularly want to make you acquainted with." The letter was signed by his aunt, Georgina, Lady Bridgewater.

In January the Duke had had a very frank conversation with Lady Bridgewater, his father's sister. "No doubt it will be somewhat difficult to find a combination of all the qualities that I require," he said to his aunt with a charming smile. "But I am sure I can rely on you, my dear Aunt, to do your best." As he had remained in Sussex and she had gone back to London, this letter was the first he had heard from her since. He took out paper to pen a note of acceptance.

Lady Bridgewater had been on the lookout for an heiress for her nephew for months when Teresa Bodmin had swum into her ken. It was not as if there were no English heiresses on the scene. There were at least three of them on the market this particular Season, but Lady Bridgewater feared that none of them would do for Adrian. There was Lady Elizabeth Osgood, but she had buck teeth and a poor complexion. There was Miss Dunleven, who was fat. And there was Miss Morrison, whose vapidity amounted to almost an affliction. Lady Bridgewater knew her nephew. He was fastidious and particular and his standard was high. Neither Lady Elizabeth nor Miss Dunleven nor Miss Morrison would do.

She was beginning to think that Teresa Bodmin would. Her birth was deplorable, of course, but the girl herself was ladylike and seemed well educated. She was extremely lovely, which was an important consideration when one was dealing with Adrian. Her father had certainly given Lady Bridgewater to understand that money would be no difficulty. And Adrian had to have money. All in all, Lady Bridgewater was inclined to think that Miss Bodmin would suit very well.

She had waited for one month before arranging a meeting between her nephew and the American girl. She had wanted to be quite sure that she had not overrated Miss Bodmin's suitability. In keeping with her purpose, Lady Bridgewater had constituted herself Tracy's unofficial chaperone and mentor, had taken her everywhere and introduced her to everyone and had watched her carefully. If this girl was called upon to fill one of the highest positions in Great Britain, Lady Bridgewater wanted to be certain she would fill it adequately.

She had been pleased by what she had seen. There was scarcely a flaw to be found in Tracy's deportment. The girl moved and spoke and gestured with all the unconscious grace one usually saw only in women of great beauty. Tracy was not a great beauty; her eyes were too widely set, her nose too short, her mouth too full, to qualify her for that category. But when one looked at Tracy, one did not notice these defects; one saw the vitality, the carefree brilliance, the vivid charm. It was generally accepted in London that she was the prettiest girl anyone had seen for quite some time.

It was a pity that she was an American, but Lady Bridgewater had decided to overlook that flaw. There was something faintly exotic in her being an American, the Duke's aunt decided. And an American was preferable to the daughter of some vulgar cit. Tracy was not vulgar. Nor was her father, though he was certainly different.

It never occurred to Lady Bridgewater to wonder if Tracy might not take kindly to the position she was being considered for so carefully. Adrian St. John Geoffrey George Deincourt was the eleventh earl and sixth duke of his line. He was twenty-six years of age, heartbreakingly handsome and utterly charming. Lady Bridgewater knew all too well the fatal attraction her nephew appeared to exercise upon her own sex. She had observed his behavior with her usual acuteness the winter before last in Paris. It had appeared to her then that Adrian had only one way of dealing with an attractive woman: he made love to her. There were quite a large number of attractive women in Paris, and while Lady Bridgewater did not hold her nephew accountable for making love to *all* of them, he certainly had done his best not to leave many out.

It was perfectly clear to Lady Bridgewater that any young lady who was offered the chance of becoming the bride of her nephew—her nephew who was as beautiful as a god; who had the bluest blood in England running through his veins; who was the Duke of Hastings, the foremost young man in England, indeed in the world—any young lady offered such a chance would thank heaven on her knees and jump at it.

Chapter 3

This is the prettiest lowborn lass that ever
Ran on the greensward.

—Shakespeare

Tracy Bodmin stifled a yawn and replied politely
to the observation of Lady Margaret Southington,
who was seated next to her on the sofa. The ladies
were all in the drawing room of Lady Margaret's
house in Grosvenor Square. The gentlemen were
still sitting over their port in the dining room. For
the last half hour Tracy had been wishing devoutly that she were in the dining room and not
the drawing room. She did not at all admire the
English custom of separating the men and women
after dinner. She found English women very hard
to talk to.

"Do you like London, Miss Bodmin?" asked her
hostess, clearly trying to find the proper way to
speak to an American.

Tracy smiled. "Everyone has been most kind to
Papa and me."

"It must be so interesting for you, meeting so

many new people and seeing so many new things,"
Lady Margaret smiled with conscious grace.

Tracy looked at that superior smile and felt a
flash of temper. The *smugness* of the English, she
thought. She had never in her life been patronized
until she had come to England.

"It is enjoyable, certainly, to see new people and
new things," she returned pleasantly. "But I guess
one always likes most what one knows best. I shall
be glad to see home again."

Lady Margaret raised a skeptical eyebrow. "You
come from Boston, I believe?"

"From Salem," said Tracy definitely.

"I am afraid I am woefully ignorant of American
geography," said Lady Margaret graciously.

"Really? I'm so sorry," said Tracy. Lady Margaret stared. It was presumably the first time she
had been condoled with on her ignorance. The
door opened and Tracy felt a surge of relief as the
gentlemen came in.

There was an empty chair next to the sofa and
three young men headed directly for it. Lord
James Belton was the victor and, sitting down, he
proceeded to do all he could to make himself
agreeable to Tracy. Tracy smiled at him, delighted
to be talking to someone who wasn't Lady Margaret. All the young men she had met in London
had been very pleasant, but then that was nothing
unusual. Tracy was used to young men who made
themselves pleasant. The fact that many of these
young men were styled "Lord" something or other
meant very little to her. The ranks and standings of
the English aristocracy were vague to her, and
peculiar as well.

Tracy was a true daughter of the American Revolution, a republican to her fingertips. She was proud of her family, proud that her father had worked his way from ship's boy to where he stood today. If truth were known, her mind was as prejudiced as those of the people with whom she was now consorting, only in the opposite direction. To Tracy there was a special virtue in being lowborn; to her mind only the self-made bore the mark of true ability. For those who lived on the wealth of their ancestors she felt something that might with some accuracy be called contempt.

However, there was not a trace of contempt in the flashing smile she turned upon Lord Belton. That young man, clearly bedazzled, pulled his chair a little closer to the sofa. "I say, you are looking awfully pretty tonight, Miss Bodmin," he said. Tracy laughed and made an appropriate reply.

Later that night, as she was preparing for bed, Tracy went over again in her mind the strangeness of her present position. She had no idea why her father had taken it into his head to come to England, nor, now that they were here, was she sure why they lingered. William Bodmin was clearly enjoying himself and clearly delighted by their reception in English society. He was, however, the kind of man who always had a purpose. It was not like him to spend his time simply in the pursuit of pleasure, yet that appeared to be what he was doing.

It was not that Tracy begrudged her father his pleasure. It was the oddity of his behavior that concerned her. And she was worried about his health as well. He had a chronic cough that she did not like, and he appeared to lose his breath far too easily. She had had no success in getting him to see a doctor. "I'm just fine, Trace," he would say heartily. "Just not as young as I used to be, that's all." Which was nonsense, to Tracy's mind. One did not, at age fifty-eight, suddenly develop a cough. But he seemed to get annoyed when she pushed him, and so she had let the matter drop. But she worried.

In most ways she was enjoying her visit to England. She was moving among people whose ways were unknown to her and she often felt like standing still and staring quietly at all of them; they seemed so unreal. But the experience was interesting, and many people—especially the young men—had gone out of their way to be friendly. She didn't exactly *approve* of the English, but she really couldn't dislike them.

And there was one area in which she admitted, without reservation, that they excelled over Americans. Tracy had a great love for, and an enormous appreciation of, the written word. It was tremendously exciting for her to think that she was in the very country that had produced writers like William Shakespeare and John Milton and Samuel Johnson. Samuel Coleridge, whom she idolized, was actually living in London at the present time, and it was Tracy's fondest hope that she might meet him. She had recently been reading a newly published poem by a hitherto unknown poet: it was called *Endymion: A Poetic Romance*, and Tracy was in ecstasy about it and about the author,

Mr. John Keats. She thought she could forgive much of a nation that produced writers like these.

She picked up *Endymion* now as she got into bed. Her mind was uneasy and she turned, from long habit, to the never failing magic of literature. She read for half an hour and then put out her light and went to sleep.

She had a visit the following afternoon that seriously ruffled the tranquillity of her feelings toward the English. She and her father were staying at the Clarendon Hotel and Tracy was sitting by herself reading in the drawing room of their suite when Lord Belton was announced. No unmarried English lady would dream of receiving a gentleman caller unchaperoned, but Tracy was not an English lady and was accustomed to speaking and walking with a young gentleman just as she might with another young lady. So she put her book down and smiled as Lord Belton came into the room.

That young man took the hand she offered and stood for a moment gazing into her face. Tracy recovered her hand gently but decidedly. "Why are you not at your club, Lord Belton?" she asked. "I thought all English gentlemen spent the day at their clubs."

"I had much rather come to see you," said Lord Belton simply. Really, he thought, as he took a deep breath and prepared to take the plunge, really she was quite the prettiest girl he had ever seen.

"That is very nice of you," she was saying. "May I give you some tea, Lord Belton?"

"No." They were by this time sitting opposite each other on the long sofa. "Actually, Miss Bodmin, I have come here with a definite purpose in mind. It is to tell you how much I love you, so much in fact that I wish to make you my wife."

There was a little pause. "I thank you for your admiration, Lord Belton," said Tracy at last. "I am honored. But I cannot be your wife."

The young man moved closer to her on the sofa and managed to possess himself of her hand. "Do not say that!" he said earnestly. "Of course there will be some little fuss about it, your being an American, I mean, but no one will hold it against you, I assure you."

Tracy's back stiffened. "Indeed?"

"I have a very good income of my own. I want you to know that I am not interested in your money."

"Indeed?" said Tracy again.

"I can give you as good a position as any man in England. You will be Lady Belton."

"Lord Belton," Tracy said with dangerous calm, "I rather think that wherever I am, I can make a position for myself. I am Tracy Bodmin. I do not need you to lend me countenance."

"Of course you do not!" said Lord Belton hastily, conscious at last that he had erred. "I did not mean that personally you lacked for anything. I simply meant to say that I can make an English lady out of you."

"You have said quite enough, Lord Belton." Tracy rose to her feet and stared at the young man, her eyes flashing. "I am an American citizen and that is quite good enough for me. I have no desire to aspire to the heights of being an English lady."

"Miss Bodmin, you have mistaken my meaning . . ." said Lord Belton miserably.

"Perhaps I have. However, let you not mistake mine. I do not wish to marry you, sir. You may take your title and your income elsewhere." And she rang the bell.

"And is this all the answer I am to have?" he asked, beginning to look angry.

"You have asked me a question and I have replied," said Tracy. "You will find consolation enough in the future when you realize the horrors I have spared you." The waiter from the hotel came in and Tracy said, "Lord Belton is leaving."

Lord Belton picked up his hat, looked unhappily at Tracy's implacable face and left.

Tracy had not completely recovered her tranquillity by the time she and her father were leaving for Lady Bridgewater's reception that evening. There was no doubt at all in Tracy's mind that she was one of the best, and she resented fiercely Lord Belton's implication that marriage to him would raise her in the eyes of the world. It was all part of the smug patronage she had detected in the English attitude toward Americans. It was not an attitude that Tracy appreciated.

However, she said nothing to her father about Lord Belton's proposal. One of the things that was beginning to disturb her most was the suspicion that her father would agree with Lord Belton's assessment of the situation, not with hers. And she was also afraid that her father would not regard with the same disdain as she a proposal of marriage from Lord Belton, a man whom Tracy would not have considered marrying even had he been an American. He was good looking enough, she supposed, but stupid. Compared to Adam Lancaster he was uninteresting indeed.

Chapter 4

The courtier, therefore, beside nobleness of
birth I will have him to be fortunate in this
behalf, and by nature to have not only a wit
and a comely shape of person and countenance,
but also a certain grace, and, as they say, a hue
that shall make him at the first sight acceptable
and loving unto whoso beholdeth him.
    —*Castiglione, the Book of the Courtier*

Lady Bridgewater's reception was not as large as
Tracy had anticipated. Her experience with London social functions had been that they were generally conducted on a massive scale. A reception
for a mere fifty or so people seemed very small. As
she caught herself thinking this, Tracy was conscious of a flash of amusement. Until her visit to
London her idea of a big social function had been a
subscription ball for 150 people at Hamilton Hall in
Salem. In all her previous life, she had been to but
one formal dinner, at the Derby family mansion on
Chestnut Street. Salem did not go in for a grand social life. Tracy was used to occasions like sleigh-

riding parties in winter or fishing parties in the bay in summer. Society, as it was conducted in London, had been a revelation to her.

Lady Bridgewater greeted the Bodmins with a warm smile and looked with particular approval at Tracy. The girl, she thought, was always immaculately groomed. Tracy seemed to have the knack of looking just right no matter what the occasion. Her clothing was simple, elegant and expensive.

This evening she was wearing a gown of lemon-yellow Italian silk that served to bring out the blonde in her hair. She wore an exquisite string of matched pearls around her neck, and pearl-encrusted combs held her hair back from her temples. That hair was allowed to fall in a seemingly careless tumble of silky curls almost to her shoulders. Lady Bridgewater had no doubt that Tracy's distinctive look of casual perfection took hard hours of preparation, but the result was always fresh and delightful.

"I am happy to see you this evening, my dear," Lady Bridgewater said kindly. "I have not planned anything too elaborate—just a gathering of a few friends." What Lady Bridgewater did not say was that those friends were the *crème de la crème* of English society, that people would be willing to kill for an invitation to one of these "gatherings of a few friends," that the inclusion of the Bodmins was occasioning a great deal of comment.

Tracy, completely oblivious to the honor she had been accorded, smiled back at Lady Bridgewater and went with her father to speak to the Princesse de Lieven. About fifteen minutes later, as Tracy was speaking to Lord Morehouse, a little rustle of electricity ran around the room, and Tracy automatically looked around. The disturbance seemed to be caused by a young man who was standing in the doorway speaking to Lady Bridgewater. As Tracy watched, he offered his arm to the Countess and they advanced together into the room. They stopped for a moment to speak to Mrs. Nesbet and her daughter, who both curtsied.

"Who is that?" Tracy asked Lord Morehouse curiously.

"That, my dear young lady, is Lady Bridgewater's nephew, the Duke of Hastings. No one has seen very much of him since he came back from Paris last winter after his father's death. He must have come up to London for her ladyship's reception." Lord Morehouse was watching the Duke as well. "One has always heard of him, of course."

The Duke was slowly circling the room with his aunt, stopping to greet people as he progressed, and Tracy was conscious of a sudden feeling that the room had expanded, had become higher and wider and more appointed for greatness, for occasions of state and royalty. It was an odd impression to receive from the mere sight of a slender young man, however good looking he might be, at a reception.

Resolutely, she went back to talking to Lord Morehouse. Ten minutes later, Lady Bridgewater was at her side. "Miss Bodmin, I should like very much to introduce you to my nephew, the Duke of Hastings," she said smiling. "Adrian, may I present Miss Teresa Bodmin, of Salem, Massachusetts."

Tracy held out her hand. As a good republican she had no intention of curtseying to anyone, and most certainly not to an English aristocrat. "How do you do, Miss Bodmin?" said the Duke. "I had the pleasure of the acquaintance of your Minister in Paris, Mr. Gallatin, and I remember him speaking highly of your father. I understand you are visiting London for a few months?"

Tracy was immediately disarmed. She gave him a friendly smile. "Yes. That is, Papa and I have been here for a month now, and I haven't heard him say anything about leaving, so I guess you might say we are here for a while."

"Splendid." He smiled back at her and turned to say a few words to include Lord Morehouse in the conversation. After another minute or so the Duke and Lady Bridgewater moved off, and Tracy saw them go up to her father, with whom they remained in conversation for at least fifteen minutes.

Ever since the Duke had come in, the atmosphere in the room had changed. Tracy sensed it, sensed that people were looking at him, sensed the respect with which people addressed him. He was a presence even though he did nothing that seemed to attract attention. He was, in fact, a slender young man of no more than average height. Adam Lancaster, who was six feet three inches at least, was physically much more imposing, thought Tracy to herself.

Half an hour later she was seated on one of the small gilt chairs talking to Sir Arthur Brett, when the Duke, this time by himself, approached them. The Duke said to Sir Arthur, "Would you mind giving me your chair so that I may talk with Miss Bodmin for a while?"

Tracy was shocked by such blatant rudeness, but

the Duke was smiling charmingly at Sir Arthur, who got up with alacrity. Evidently he was not at all put out and considered it a privilege to be able to vacate his chair for the Duke of Hastings.

"I have a very high opinion of Americans, you see," the Duke said to Tracy when he was sitting next to her, "and I take whatever opportunity I can to further my acquaintance with your countrymen."

"What Americans have you met, my lord, besides Mr. Gallatin?" Tracy asked suspiciously.

"Mr. John Quincy Adams," he replied promptly and looked at her with amusement to see what she would say.

Tracy's lips curved. Whatever would this English aristocrat have made of John Quincy Adams? "Did you have a high opinion of Mr. Adams, my lord?" she asked demurely.

"Yes," he answered immediately. "I don't say I should like to spend an extended period of time in his company,"—here Tracy involuntarily laughed— "but he has a relentlessly brilliant mind. I understand he is employed at present in the negotiation of a treaty for the Floridas. If Spain isn't careful, he will have everything else she owns on the continent as well."

Tracy was delighted. The Duke was the first English person she had talked to who seemed to know anything at all about America. He was also quite astonishingly handsome. She had never seen eyes of so dark a blue. "Mr. Adams is not a . . . comfortable . . . kind of person, I am afraid," she returned. "But Papa shares your opinion of his brilliance." She looked at him appraisingly. "General Jackson has headed up an expedition into Florida, you know. The Spanish government is bound by treaty to keep the Indians at peace with the United States, and they have failed to do so."

He looked suddenly stern. "Ah, yes, General Jackson. Another of your singularly competent countrymen."

"Do you know, my lord," Tracy said candidly, "I have found that most English people have never even heard of Andrew Jackson?"

His face did not relax. "I rather wish that I had not heard of him, Miss Bodmin," he replied. "I knew quite a few chaps who did not come back from New Orleans."

"I'm sorry," Tracy said softly. She sighed. "It was a silly war, really."

"Well, it is over now and so we can be friends." His blue eyes smiled at her. "I do so hope we are going to be friends, Miss Bodmin," he said softly.

"I hope so, too," Tracy replied, fascinated. Then her brow puckered slightly. "Do you know, I haven't the slightest idea of how I should address you. The protocol of the English aristocracy has quite eluded my grasp, I fear."

"The proper term of address for a duke is 'Your Grace,'" he replied serenely.

Tracy smiled, eyes crinkling and teeth gleaming. "Really?"

"However, I would not ask so much of a good republican like youself. 'My Lord' will do admirably."

"I am so glad," she replied with faint irony and he grinned, looking all of a sudden charmingly boyish.

"May I call on you tomorrow?"

"Yes, you may," said Tracy Bodmin, that ardent republican.

"Well?" said Lady Bridgewater to her nephew after the last of her guests had gone and they were alone together in the empty saloon. She had seen the attention that Adrian had paid to Tracy, but that attention did not necessarily mean anything conclusive. The Duke paid attention to a pretty girl in much the same manner as he would listen to a piece of well-played music. Attention, in each case, was what he considered simple good manners.

He looked at her for a minute without speaking. Then he smiled slightly. "Yes," he said. "I think she'll do."

Tracy went home with her father, unaware that she had just passed a momentous test. "I liked that Duke of Hastings," her father said as they were sitting side by side in their carriage.

"Did you, Papa? Evidently he is quite a *grand seigneur* over here."

"The grandest. Next best thing to royalty, according to Lord Melrose."

"Yet he seemed to know quite a bit about America."

"Yes, I discovered that myself. We had a very interesting discussion about the British Navigation Laws."

Tracy looked startled. "Did you?"

"Yes." Tracy could hear from his voice that her father was smiling. "That is, *I* talked about the Navigation Laws, and he listened. But he did actu-

ally listen, which is rare for an Englishman in regard to that topic."

"Yes."

Her father turned to her. "You liked him, didn't
you, Trace?"

"I'm afraid I did."

"Why afraid?"

"I shouldn't mind if I didn't," she said, with
truth if not with great rationality. "Falling like
that, in twenty minutes, so utterly into his hands—
it's not good for a girl's pride."

"Nonsense," replied her father, very pleased with
her answer. "What has pride to do with it?"

The Duke came to call the next day and sat talking to Tracy for over an hour. The day after that
he took her driving in the park, and later in the
week he escorted both Bodmins and Lady Bridgewater to the theatre.

He was very pleased with his aunt's protégée. If
he had been given his own choice, he would have
chosen his bride from his own order, a girl who
would understand the duties and responsibilities of
the great position she would be called upon to fill.
But he did not have freedom of choice. Nor could
he look with anything but pleasure at this American girl whom he proposed to make his wife.

She was different from any girl he had ever met.
She looked at him frankly, her sunny head not
tilted in coquetry when she spoke or listened, but
serenely upright. He liked looking at her, at her
eyes, so brilliantly hazel, the whites so ultra white,
at her short straight nose, her glowing skin, her
wide, full mouth. There was passion in that mouth,

he thought, and intelligence in her eyes. He did not think it would be difficult for her to learn the things she had not been bred to.

At the end of two weeks, the Duke invited Mr. and Miss Bodmin to visit his estate, Steyning Castle, in Sussex. The only other persons included in the invitation were Lord and Lady Bridgewater. It was as good as a proposal of marriage, and Mr. Bodmin knew it even if Tracy did not.

William Bodmin had, by this time, managed to find out a great deal about the Duke of Hastings. At first it had not seemed possible to the American that such a personage as the Duke could be seriously interested in Tracy. Mr. Bodmin had looked into the history of the Deincourt family. He had seen for himself the dignity of the Duke's position. That his daughter should be a duchess! In his wildest dreams, Mr. Bodmin had not hoped for so much.

But he had had a very interesting conversation with Lady Bridgewater in which it had become apparent that the state of the ducal finances left a great deal to be desired. Mr. Bodmin had told her ladyship when first they met that he wanted the best article on the market for his girl, and it now appeared that that was what he was being offered. He would never dream of forcing a match on Tracy that she would not like, but Mr. Bodmin was certain that she did like the Duke of Hastings.

The Bodmins accepted the Duke's gracious invitation and planned to go down to Steyning Castle at the end of May.

Chapter 5

For nobleness of birth is, as it were, a clear
lamp that sheweth forth and bringeth into light
works both good and bad.
                              —*The Book of the Courtier*

Three days before they left for Steyning Castle
something happened that would radically affect the
outcome of that visit. Tracy was arranging flowers
in the small breakfast room that was really an alcove off the drawing room of their suite when the
door opened and her father and Richard Rush
came in. Tracy did not immediately make her
presence known but went on putting the finishing
touches to her arrangement. She had no intention
of eavesdropping, but when she realized what the
two men were talking about, that is exactly what
she did.

The beginning of their conversation was
harmless. "Congress has closed American ports to
all British vessels arriving from a colony that is le-
gally closed to American ships," said Mr. Rush. "I

just received notice from Mr. Adams. It won't go down well with the English."

"It is Britain's fault for not allowing America to export to the West Indies. The West Indian planters are as angry as we are about the present situation. England must be made to realize that she cannot monopolize the trade; she must be made to realize that her Navigation Laws are archaic."

"Mr. Adams writes me that he sees our action as a test, a contest between American nationalism and British mercantilism." There was a pause. "I wonder, Mr. Bodmin, if you would care to speak to the British government on this issue? As the single largest shipowner in America, your words would have some weight."

"I would be glad to speak to Lord Castlereagh, but you must not count on me, Rush. I will be going home very shortly now."

This was when Tracy's head jerked up and she really began to listen.

"I did not know that," said Richard Rush. "Perhaps I might ask you to be my ambassador to Mr. Adams in Washington?"

"I cannot promise to go to Washington, Rush," said Mr. Bodmin heavily. "I shall be glad to make it just to Salem." He paused, then said quite kindly, "I am dying, you see."

"What!"

"Yes, I am dying. The doctor gave me six months when I left home."

"My dear Bodmin," said Richard Rush, clearly distressed. "I had no idea."

"No one has, not even my daughter. I only tell you because I want to ask a favor of you."

"Anything, my dear fellow."

"I will be going home, but I rather think Tracy will be staying. The Duke of Hastings has invited us to visit his home in Sussex and I expect a proposal of marriage to be forthcoming."

"The Duke of Hastings!" Mr. Rush was clearly overwhelmed.

"Yes. Tracy knows nothing of my illness and I don't want her to know. It may be selfish of me, but I want her to remember me as a man of strength and vigor, not as a rasping, coughing husk of a thing. I will not tell her." He leaned forward. "I will no longer be here, but I should like to think that Tracy has a friend in you, Rush."

"Of course I will be her friend," Richard Rush said warmly.

Mr. Bodmin nodded, apparently satisfied. "It will perhaps be a little difficult for her at first, accustoming herself to English ways. She will feel better if there is another American she can look to."

Shortly after that, the American Minister left and Mr. Bodmin walked slowly to his bedroom. Tracy stayed in the breakfast room for twenty more minutes, her body rigid with shock, her knuckles white with tension as they grasped the back of a chair.

She had known something was wrong with her father, but she had had no idea of its seriousness. He was dying! And he did not want her to know. He wanted her to marry an English duke and let him go home to die alone.

Everything in Tracy rebelled at the thought. If he was to die, she must be there to comfort him and nurse him in his final hours. She would not let him leave alone.

But as she stood, rigid, staring blindly at the flowers she had just been arranging so carefully, her father's words seemed to sound again in the room. He did not want her to know. He did not want her to hold his hand, to nurse him and care for him. It came to her as she stood there, fighting a great battle within herself, that the greatest comfort she could give him was to pretend ignorance and let him go. He was a very proud man; she had always known that. He had never yet been beaten at anything. He would not want her to watch his final defeat.

But to marry the Duke of Hastings! Such a thought had never crossed Tracy's mind. She did not know if, even to please her father, she could bring herself to do that. If he were anxious to see her married and taken care of, why would Adam Lancaster not do as well?

The visit to Steyning Castle was consequently fraught with tension and emotion beneath its surface pleasantness. The house was enormous, with two battlemented towers, a royal gateway and vestiges of a moat as evidence that it had at one time been a fortified castle indeed. A multitude of additions over the years had somewhat softened its martial look, however, and today, with the Duke's flag flying, it looked merely grand and impressive but not awesome.

The Duke had offered to show the Bodmins around and Mr. Bodmin had accepted with alacrity. It was plain to see, as they paraded from room to room, that he was enjoying himself enormously. He could not hear enough of how the Castle had been held by the Deincourts since the thirteenth century, of how the royal coat of arms over the gate and the inscription *Dom Rex Henricus Octav* had been put there for a welcome to King Henry VIII on one of his visits, of how Henry, his daughter Elizabeth and Kings James I and Charles I had all slept in the state bedroom, of how Cromwell's soldiers had stolen the royal gilt bed . . . The Duke remarked several times that he hoped he was not boring his guests with all this family history, but it was clearly obvious that Mr. Bodmin, at any rate, was hanging on his every word.

Tracy was more interested in the house than in the Duke's ancestors. She had thought Samuel McIntire had built the Bodmins a grand house on Chestnut Street in Salem, but she had never in her life seen anything like Steyning Castle.

It had a fifteenth-century Great Hall with a hammerbeam ceiling, a great seventeenth-century fireplace and a magnificent stone minstrels' gallery. The drawing room had an Elizabethan plasterwork ceiling and elaborate wood paneling.

"My grandfather had Robert Adam rearrange and redo the house," the Duke said as they passed along a stunning marble-floored gallery that ran for fully eighty feet. "He added this wing, which also contains the library, and a wing for the servants." As he finished speaking he led the way into the library and Tracy involuntarily gasped.

"How many books do you have, my lord?" she asked reverently, her eyes going over the shelves and shelves of tooled-leather volumes.

"About ten thousand," he replied and Tracy felt her jaw drop.

After dinner they all strolled outdoors on the lush, smooth lawn that was punctuated by ponds and copses of trees. The fish pond was what was left of the moat, the Duke told them. "The first duke and his sons fought strenuously for the king during the Civil War and Cromwell only let them return to the house on the condition that the moat was filled in and the battlements made useless."

Mr. Bodmin was content as he went to bed that first night. He had got what he wanted for his girl. The flavor of success had always been highly agreeable to him, and it had been his luck to know it often. But it had never before been so sweet, been associated with so much that was gracious and ancient and valuable. The thought of his girl living in a house like this; of his grandchildren—his blood—growing up here, belonging here; made him feel that he—William Bodmin, a cottage boy from Cornwall—had done very well indeed.

Tracy had met the Duke's young sister and brother at tea the day before, but they had not been at dinner. When she came downstairs for breakfast in the morning, she found both brothers addressing themselves heartily to a substantial meal. They both wore riding clothes.

The Duke rose as soon as he saw her, and Harry followed suit quickly. "What a nice surprise," the Duke said, with a charming smile.

Tracy seated herself. "Why a surprise? Have I done the wrong thing by coming down?"

"Not at all," he assured her. "It is just that we

males very rarely see a woman at the breakfast table. Most ladies prefer to breakfast upstairs in bed."

"In bed?" Tracy looked astonished. The only time she had ever eaten in bed was when she was sick. Privately, she thought the whole practice sounded decadent. "Well, I hope you won't mind if I join you?"

"We are delighted," said the Duke and put aside the paper he had been reading.

"Do go on with your paper," she said. Harry went to pick up his, and the Duke frowned slightly. Harry put it back down. "As a matter of fact," Tracy said as she helped herself to a plate of food, "I'd enjoy a look at a paper myself."

"You can have part of mine, Miss Bodmin," Harry said generously. "I only read the parts about horses anyway."

Tracy gave him a friendly smile and accepted his offer. Silence fell as the three of them sipped their coffee and perused their papers. "Ah ha," said the Duke after about ten minutes, "I see where your country has closed its ports to British vessels."

Tracy put down her paper. "What does your article say?" He read it to her and Tracy's lips curved in disdain. "Really, my lord, why is your government so indignant? What did they expect? There is a natural exchange between American tobacco, rice, grain, beans and flour and West Indian rum, molasses and coffee. What Britain has said is that there is to be no trade between the West Indies and the United States unless it is done through Britain. That is unacceptable to us. So we have responded: if you will not allow us to trade with the

West Indies, we will not allow *you* to trade with us."

"You did something like that to us before, if I remember correctly," he said slowly.

"Yes. The Embargo of 1807. And according to my father, the embargo wreaked havoc on the British economy."

"Did it indeed?" he asked thoughtfully.

"Yes, it did." She smiled a little ruefully. "To be frank, it didn't do our economy any good, either."

He looked at her levelly. "All this is very interesting. I freely confess that I am abysmally ignorant of the international trading picture, but I am also willing to learn. Being a good Britisher, I do realize that trade is what makes the world revolve."

At that she grinned. "Good heavens, my lord, you sound like Papa!"

He sipped his coffee. "I consider that a compliment," he said tranquilly. "Your father is a very astute man."

There was a pause and into it Harry spoke cautiously, "Are you riding over to Winchelsea this morning, Adrian?"

"Yes. Should you care to accompany me, Miss Bodmin?"

Tracy shook her head. "I think, if you don't mind, I will spend the morning in your library."

"You must do whatever you please," he responded. "I hope, however, that it will please you to drive out with me for a little this afternoon?"

"That would be lovely," said Tracy.

"May I go with you to Winchelsea, Adrian?" Harry asked eagerly.

His brother looked at him dampeningly. "I

thought you worked with your tutor in the morning?"

"I will work twice as hard this afternoon," Harry assured him earnestly.

The Duke sighed. "Oh, very well. Will you excuse us, Miss Bodmin?"

"Certainly. Enjoy your ride." She went back to her paper and, out of the corner of her eye, watched the brothers leave the room. Harry did not greatly resemble the Duke. He had red-blond hair, light blue eyes and freckles. He was also, at fourteen, an inch or so taller than his elder brother. But he did not have the Duke's character. Tracy was quite certain that at age fourteen the Duke had already had the air of regal distinction that was so much a part of his personality today. It was an air that one could not but find impressive, no matter how much one might diapprove of it in theory.

Chapter 6

What say you? Can you love the gentleman?
                                    —Shakespeare

The Duke looked with obvious pleasure at his guest when she joined him that afternoon for their appointed drive. Tracy deserved the appreciation; she was looking lovely in a dress of lime-green cambric with a little jacket and a hat that perched dashingly on the side of her curly head. The skirt was cut close to her body and showed off her elegant slenderness to admiration. As the Duke watched her walk toward him, he thought to himself that he had always liked best a long-legged woman.

No hint of this private observation appeared on his handsome face, however, as he greeted Tracy and helped her into his phaeton. Without seeming to look at all, he also ascertained that she had splendid ankles.

The Duke was pleased more than ever with Miss Bodmin. Any woman who did not expect to be entertained at the breakfast table was a pearl beyond price in his view. He had every intention of speaking to Mr. Bodmin before dinner this evening. His own code of conduct would not allow him to approach Tracy until he had her father's sanction, but he had little doubt that that sanction would be forthcoming.

Meanwhile, his plan for the afternoon was to charm Tracy. He was a man who had known many women and his personal magnetism, when he chose to exert it, was enormous. She knew what he was doing, having been forewarned by what she had heard in London of the probable reason for this visit, and thought that she did not want to marry him, and yet—she was charmed. But, even while she felt the power of his spell and felt the pleasure she took in his presence sweep all her defenses away, she felt a sort of apprehension at the weaknesses he produced in her.

They were driving along a narrow path through the estate woods when they turned a corner to find a tree down across their path. The Duke pulled the horses up abruptly, then turned to Tracy. "Are you all right, Miss Bodmin?"

"I'm fine," she assured him. She looked at the obstacle in their path. "However did that get there?"

"It must have come down in a storm. Can you hold the horses while I take a closer look?" She assented and he handed her the reins, vaulting lightly to the ground. He went over to the obstacle. "It's a dead branch," he said, coming back to the phaeton. "There is no way I can turn the horses on this narrow path. I'll have to get it out of the way." He was taking off his coat as he spoke and Tracy looked at him dubiously. The branch looked very heavy and he was not a big man.

"Are you sure you can't turn around?" she asked.

"Yes," he replied briefly and handed her his jacket. He looked a great deal stronger in his shirt sleeves than Tracy had expected. He advanced to the tree branch and bent over, lifting it up off the road. Tracy could see his back muscles ripple through the thin fabric of his shirt. He moved the branch to the side of the path with little difficulty, dusted his hands together and came back to the phaeton. He accepted his coat from Tracy and said, "I'll send someone out here to get rid of it entirely." It was still protruding a little onto the road because the trees grew so closely together that there was not space to throw it entirely into the wood.

He took the reins back from Tracy and as he turned toward her she noticed a light beading of sweat on his forehead. Without thinking, she put up her hand and lightly touched his brow with her forefinger. "Sweat!" she said teasingly. "I did not know that dukes could sweat."

He did not answer but looked back at her, suddenly intent, his eyes narrowing. Tracy was abruptly aware of their isolation, of the cool green woods all around them, of the silence. He was going to kiss her, she thought, and her heart began to hammer. It seemed as if he moved toward her but then he checked, like a man on the brink of an unexpected cliff. He turned to the horses. "Oh, yes," he said, as he put the team into motion. "A duke is, after all, only a man, Miss Bodmin."

Tracy didn't answer, and after a moment he began to talk of something else.

The Duke invited Mr. Bodmin into his study that afternoon and broached the topic that was the reason for the Bodmin's visit. "I should very much like, Mr. Bodmin," the Duke said calmly, "to marry your daughter."

Mr. Bodmin leaned back in his chair and stretched his legs. "I won't pretend that this is a surprise, Your Grace," he replied. "There are, however, a few questions I want to ask you before I give you my answer."

The Duke nodded. "Certainly."

"I want, first, to tell you about Tracy's parents. I was a poor cottage boy from a fishing village in Cornwall. I went to America when I was thirteen, I worked hard, and I made my fortune. I am a very rich man and in America I am both esteemed and honored, but I am not like your people. My dear wife was the daughter of a poor Irish lad from County Kerry, who came to America, like me, and, like me, also made a fortune. She was solid gold, but she was not a lady in your sense of the word." Mr. Bodmin leaned a little forward. "Now, what I want to know, Duke, is if Tracy, the daughter of such parents as I have described to you, will be accepted by your friends as their equal. Will all those countesses and earls and marquises accept her and welcome her as your wife, as your duchess?"

"She will be accepted, Mr. Bodmin. I know what you are saying, and I will not hide from you the fact that such a marriage is bound to occasion comment, but she will most certainly be accepted." The Duke smiled. "There is a brightness and a grace about Tracy which would ensure her acceptance in any society, I believe."

Mr. Bodmin nodded with pleasure and the Duke went on gravely. "If you fear that this would be an unequal marriage from the point of view of birth, I must tell you, Mr. Bodmin, that it would also be unequal from the point of view of fortune. You say you are a very rich man. I am not."

"The land you own must be worth a fortune," Mr. Bodmin said.

"There are mortgages on nearly everything. If the mortgages were cleared and money put into the land instead of wrung out of it, then, sir, the land would indeed be worth a fortune. Painful for me as it is, I must admit that my father and grandfather were not good stewards of their property. The result of their profligacy is my own near bankruptcy."

The American was looking at him out of keenly narrowed eyes. "If you were to come into a fortune, Duke, how would you use it?"

"I would put it into my estates," the young man replied promptly. He looked straight at Mr. Bodmin, his dark blue eyes very serious. "*I* am not a profligate, Mr. Bodmin."

The two men looked at each other for fully ten seconds, then Tracy's father said slowly, "No, Your Grace, I don't believe you are." He sat back in his chair. "You may speak to Tracy, my lord Duke. It will be up to her. If she agrees to marry you, I am sure that my lawyers and your man of business will be able to work out a satisfactory financial arrangement."

Tracy had spent the hour that her father and the Duke were discussing her future in the stables with her proposed brother- and sister-in-law. Lord Harry, with the air of giving her a great treat, had invited her down to the stables to see his horse, and once there they had encountered Lady Mary. The two young people had shown Tracy all around the stables, which were immaculate, with stalls for at least forty horses. Most of the stalls, however, were empty.

As Tracy listened to the two youngsters chatter away she began to get a sinking feeling at the pit of her stomach. It seemed the whole Deincourt family was horse mad.

"Does your brother like to ride?" she asked Lord Harry.

"Adrian? Like to ride?" Harry stared at her as if she could not be serious. "He is the best rider I ever saw. He was in the cavalry, you know. Had three horses shot out from under him at Waterloo." Harry rarely missed an opportunity to mention this fact.

"I didn't know he had been at Waterloo," said Tracy. The Duke was far more reticent about his exploits than his admiring cadet.

"You didn't!" Harry thought the whole world knew that.

Lady Mary said disgustedly, "Adrian is not such a braggart as you, Harry."

Tracy laughed. "Well, as Lord Harry is bragging about someone else, we really cannot accuse him of conceit."

"True." Mary smiled at Tracy. The Duke's sister was very like him, with the same dark blue eyes and dark brown hair. Mary was aware, as was every living creature at Steyning Castle, that this American girl was likely to be the next duchess. Mary was determined to like her, and from what she had seen of Tracy so far, it did not appear that that task would be too difficult. "Perhaps you would care to ride with us tomorrow?" said Mary, diffidently.

"Oh dear," said Tracy, "I suppose I will have to confess. I don't ride."

Two pairs of blue eyes, one dark and one light, stared at her in consternation. There was an appalled silence. Then Mary said, "But you didn't seem to be afraid when we showed you the horses."

Tracy's eyes flashed. "I did not say I was afraid of horses, Lady Mary. I said I did not ride them. I never learned, you see."

"But how did you get around?" Harry was obviously dumbfounded.

"By boat, mostly. I grew up on the coast of Massachusetts, Lord Harry. I can sail just about anything that floats. Can you?"

"No," said Lord Harry. Tracy raised an eyebrow and he gave her a reluctant grin. "I'll tell you what, Miss Bodmin," he offered generously, "I'll teach you how to ride if you teach me how to sail."

Tracy grinned back. "That sounds a fair bargain." The three of them left the stables, harmony restored, and Tracy did not think even privately to herself that it would be unlikely that she and Lord Harry would have an opportunity to further their friendship.

The Duke had no opportunity to speak to Tracy that evening. She excused herself immediately after dinner and went to her room, saying she had letters to write. In reality, she was confused about her own feelings and wanted time to think before she was confronted by the proposal of marriage she was now positive was in the offing. She made no attempt to write a letter and was sitting in her lovely bedroom looking out the window at the twilight when there came a knock on the door and her father's voice said, "Tracy?"

"Come in, Papa," she called.

Mr. Bodmin entered the room and came across to the window where she was seated. "I didn't think you wanted to write letters," he said with a little quirk of his eyebrow.

She smiled faintly and looked up searchingly at him. He turned away to cough and when he looked back at her she thought that he had turned gray. "Sit down, Papa." She gestured to another chair and he slowly lowered his tall frame into it.

"Do you like the Duke, Tracy?" he asked directly.

"Yes, Papa, I do."

"I had a chat with him this afternoon," Mr. Bodmin went on, watching her closely. "He asked me for permission to address you."

Tracy's eyes had turned a grass green. "And what did you say, Papa?"

"I said it would be up to you, that if you wanted to marry him, I would agree to the match." She did not say anything and he went on, "I spoke to him of my concern for your happiness should you accept him and find yourself rejected by the English aristocracy as not fit to go amongst them as their

equal. He assured me that you would not be rejected, that your position would be secure to you."

"A Duchess of Hastings must always be accepted, I suppose, no matter what her background," Tracy said, keeping strict control over
her voice.

"He made no mention of your future position in
his reply," Mr. Bodmin said gravely. "His words
were 'There is a brightness and a grace about Tracy
that would ensure her acceptance in any society.' "

Tracy smiled a little ruefully. "He is certainly a
formidable young man."

"He is a kind of young man you have not met
before. We do not have young men like that in
America."

There was unmistakable admiration in Mr. Bodmin's voice and Tracy said simply, "Would it
please you to see me the wife of such a man,
Papa?"

"Yes, it would," came the unhesitating reply.

"Why?"

"He represents a way of life I admire very
much," said Mr. Bodmin, and his eyes went to the
window, to the wide, flawless lawn that stretched
away below him. "When I think of my own life, I
realize that my sole aim has always been to make
money. I was successful, but I was always so
occupied with earning money that I had very little
opportunity to reflect upon its uses. What might
one do with a life into which one has succeeded in
introducing a fortune? I look around here and I see
the kind of life that understands the uses of money,
not just the making of it. I see grace and beauty and

learning." His eyes turned back from the window and rested on his daughter.

"It is the kind of life I want for you, Tracy. You are not like me or like your dear mother either. You have been given a good education. You have an understanding of things like art and music and literature. I would like to see you given an opportunity to let those parts of you grow and flower as they would not in the America of today."

"When I used to think of marriage, I thought of a man very different from the Duke," she said hesitantly.

"You thought of Adam Lancaster, no doubt," said Mr. Bodmin and Tracy flushed a little. "I have not a word to say against Adam, Tracy, and if he is the man you love I will welcome him as my son. But Adam is too like me. In his own mind, the only reason he was born was to wrest a fortune out of the world. And I have no doubt he will do it—he is well on the way, I should think. But, like me, he has no idea of how to use it when once it has been won."

Tracy had been listening to him very seriously, but as he concluded, she flashed a smile. "Confess now, Papa. You would love to see your daughter a duchess and your future grandson a duke."

He grinned. "I would," he admitted. "But it is up to you, Tracy. My feelings do not enter into this question at all. You are to do what will make *you* happy."

"I will think about all you have said, Papa," she replied softly, and he rose from his chair, kissed her good night and went off to his own room.

Chapter 7

I might call him
A thing divine, for nothing natural
I ever saw so noble.

—Shakespeare

Tracy slept very little that night. She went over
and over again what her father had told her. "My
feelings do not enter into this question at all," he
had said, but of course they did. Knowing what
she now knew, it was more important than ever
that she do what would make him happy. She
would have few, if any, chances to please him in
the future.

Tracy was very fond of her father although she
did not know him all that well. It was true what
he had said to her tonight: all his energy and time
had gone into making his fortune. As a child she
had seen very little of him: it was her mother who
had brought her up. Then, after her mother had
died, she had gone away to the Bradford Academy,
where she had indeed received an excellent education. It was only in the six months that she had

lived at home since leaving school that she had really ever seen a great deal of her father. But she cared for him and, especially now, she desired to please him.

Then there was Adam Lancaster. She had not said she would marry him, but she had said she would listen to him after she returned from England and she had let him kiss her. It had been very pleasant, that kiss, and she had thought Adam the most impressive man she had ever seen. She lay in bed now, trying to recall his strong, dark-skinned features, his flashing brown eyes, but his face would not materialize for her. She kept seeing instead the dark blue eyes and aristocratic face of someone very different from Adam Lancaster.

The Duke was nothing in comparison to Adam, she told herself. Why, Adam had shoulders that would fill a doorway. But her mind's eye kept seeing a very different figure, a man whose shoulders were surprisingly wide and strong, even if they would not fill a doorway, a man who moved with a grace and precision she had seen on no one else, a man who, she suspected, had always gotten what he wanted. And now he wanted her.

One of the questions that bothered Tracy was *why* did he want her? She might not agree with the English prejudice about birth, but she acknowledged that the prejudice existed and would have to be coped with by both sides of the marriage that was being proposed to her. Why would a man like the Duke want to marry a girl such as herself—a girl not of noble birth, a girl who had no idea of what might be required of an English duchess?

She remembered the one other proposal of marriage she had received from an English nobleman. "I am not interested in your money," Lord Belton had said. Tracy wondered if the Duke was. From the luxury of his house it seemed impossible that he could want money. But Tracy remembered the empty stalls. She recalled Lady Mary's sad words about "the horses that had to be sold after Papa died." It was not at all unlikely, she concluded, that money was an important consideration in the Duke's choice of a wife. Tracy determined she would ask him; she did not at all care for the idea of being married for her money.

The Duke did not delay. He appeared in the library the next morning shortly after Tracy herself had settled into a comfortable chair. "May I interrupt you, Miss Bodmin?" he asked quietly, crossing the room toward her.

"Of course, my lord." Tracy put down her book and looked up gravely at him. He stood between her and the window, so that the sun coming in shone on his brown hair, which glinted with a copper sheen she had not noticed before. He looked perfectly relaxed and the thought crossed her mind that he had probably never assumed an awkward posture in his life.

"I have a confession to make," he said. "I invited you to Steyning Castle for a purely selfish reason. I wanted to show you my home. I wanted you to meet my family. I wanted, in effect, to show you the whole picture before I asked you a question that is very important to my happiness." He smiled a little wryly. "All this is a very long-winded way of saying that I find I love you and hope very much that you will be my wife."

She was looking at him very seriously. "I do not know," she replied slowly.

He came a little closer. "That is encouraging. If you are open to persuasion, let me persuade you."

She smiled a little. "I wonder if you could?"

"I shall certainly try. What is it that worries you?"

"Why do you want to marry me, my lord? I, an American with merely workaday red blood in my veins?"

"The answer to that question should be obvious to anyone with eyes," he returned, faintly smiling. She said nothing, merely watched his face. After a moment, the Duke went on. "What is *really* bothering you, Tracy?"

It was the first time he had ever used her name. Tracy looked at him directly, her eyes dark with an unreadable expression, and said, "Money."

"Ah." He did not look at all discomposed. "Do you think I wish to marry you because your father is rich?"

It was Tracy who betrayed restlessness. She rose to her feet and walked to the beautiful Adam chimney piece. Once there, she turned to face him, the width of the room between them. "Do you?" she asked baldly.

"No." He was not smiling now. "I do not deny the fact that I could not marry a woman who had no money. My father was not so clever as yours; he wasted a fortune instead of winning one. But if money were my object, there are plenty of English girls who have money. I am not asking any of them to be my wife."

He came across the room until he stood before her. "I am asking you because you are everything that is lovely and real and vital. Because you are like fresh air and sunshine. Because your eyes have the most fascinating way of changing color. Did you know, for instance, that right now they are almost gold?"

His voice had taken on a deep, caressing note that stirred her profoundly. He was trying to charm her, she thought, with his own sovereign personal power, into accepting him. "How can an American girl possibly become an English duchess?" she asked faintly, knowing she was now on the defensive.

"With the Stars and Stripes waving proudly around her," he answered and she laughed unsteadily. "Tracy," he said, and his arm went about her waist. "Say yes."

He had always thought her wide, passionate mouth was meant to be kissed and was pleased to discover that he had been right. She was inexperienced, that was clear, but after a moment she responded to him and the Duke thought that the future looked promising indeed. He raised his head. "Now they are green," he said, looking into her eyes. "Baffling."

His own eyes had turned an even darker blue, but Tracy, although she noticed, did not mention that interesting fact. "My lord," she breathed, shaken to the core by that kiss.

"Adrian," he corrected.

"Adrian," she said, and in so saying she gave him his answer.

The family and guests at Steyning Castle were all delighted with the news announced to them by the Duke during the course of the day. It was a marriage that satisfied everyone, a joining of birth and position to beauty and money. Mr. Bodmin looked forward to a line of future Dukes of Hastings with his blood running in their veins. Lady Mary and Lord Harry looked forward to filling some of those empty stalls in the stables. Lady Bridgewater looked forward to seeing the House of Deincourt, of which she still considered herself a member, restored to its rightful eminence in wealth as well as prestige.

Of all the people gathered together under the roof of Steyning Castle, the only one who had serious doubts about the felicity of the coming marriage was the prospective bride. If Adrian were an American, she thought she could then put her hand into his with a fearless heart. But in accepting him she was accepting so much more; she was accepting a way of life whose complexities and distinctions were as foreign to her as the protocol of the court of Suleiman the Magnificent. Her husband would be one of the most highly placed members of the highest aristocracy in Europe. And Tracy did not approve of aristocracy!

She would not have done it were it not for her father. She told herself, as she watched the air of achievement with which he went about the castle, that she had done the right thing. Whatever the outcome of such a marriage for her, the engagement had made her father happy.

There was one person whom it would not make happy, and Tracy had written a letter to him very shortly after she had agreed to marry the Duke. Adam Lancaster would feel she had betrayed him, and Tracy admitted to herself—as she would not ever admit to him—that he would have some justice in his complaint. Because of her guilty conscience, the letter she wrote tended to dwell rather heavily on her father's pleasure and made little mention of her own feelings.

She was not sure herself of those feelings. She would have thought a man like the Duke would have been the last kind of man in the world to attract her. He belonged to a class she distrusted. He was, in fact, an almost perfect embodiment of that class. Yet, he did attract her. He was unlike anyone she had ever met. She was not marrying him, she admitted to herself in her most honest moments, solely to please her father.

Chapter 8

Myself and what is mine to you and yours
Is now converted.

—Shakespeare

The marriage of Miss Teresa Bodmin to the Most
Noble Adrian St. John Geoffrey George Deincourt, Duke of Hastings and Marquis of Winchelsea, Earl of Hythe, Baron Deincourt of Hythe
and Baron Deincourt of Bexhill, took place at the
end of June at St. George's, Hanover Square. All
of the Deincourts were there, and all of the relations of all of the Deincourts, and all the ambassadors as well as all the Americans in London. Mr.
Bodmin wanted to see his girl married in style.
There were five bridesmaids: Lady Mary, two Deincourt cousins and two American girls from the
Ministry. Mr. Bodmin gave a sumptuous breakfast
at the Clarendon Hotel and everyone was well satisfied that the thing had been done properly.

Tracy spent the weeks before her wedding shop-
ping for clothes. The Duke's man of business came
to an extremely satisfactory arrangement with Mr.

Bodmin's lawyers. The Duke himself took his father-in-law in charge and introduced him to the exclusive domains of London clubs and parliamentary sessions. Mr. Bodmin was enormously pleased and tended to regard the Duke with an air of achieved possession that secretly amused the young man very much. Quite obviously, he was one more trophy to hang on the American's shelf. The Duke did not at all mind Mr. Bodmin's air of proprietorship. After all, he told himself, he had been expensive enough. And, too, his father-in-law was scheduled to leave for America at the beginning of July. The Duke could put up with him comfortably enough until then.

The Duke and Duchess were to take only a week's honeymoon at present, the bride desiring to be back in London in order to bid farewell to her father. The Duke owned a small estate in Hertfordshire, and it was there that they planned to spend their week. Servants had been dispatched from Steyning Castle two weeks previously, and it had been reported to the Duke that all was in readiness for his arrival.

It was a drive of several hours from London to Hertfordshire and the Duke beguiled the time for Tracy by describing to her in hilarious detail the peculiarities of the various Deincourt relations who had jammed into the church that morning. This led Tracy to expatiate a bit about her own maternal relatives, who while not so highly placed as the Duke's family were certainly as odd.

They arrived at Thorn Manor in the late afternoon. The Duke showed Tracy around while their luggage was unpacked, then they changed for dinner. As dinner progressed, Tracy felt the slight constriction that had been in her chest all day growing tighter and tighter. The Duke, seated across the table from her, was a perfect stranger, she thought. Whatever had she done?

The tightness in her chest got worse when he sent her upstairs and said he would be along in a few minutes. Her legs felt like lead as she climbed the stairs and she could not say a word to the maid who was waiting to undress her. A beautiful sheer peach-colored nightdress—a gift from Lady Bridgewater—lay on the bed. Tracy let the maid put her into the dress and brush out her hair, but all the while stark panic was rising inside her. What had she done?

Mr. Bodmin, acutely aware of the lack of a close female relative, had attempted twice to speak to his daughter about the marriage act. However, though he was a very brave man who had steered his ship through typhoons and hurricanes, he could not bring himself to talk to Tracy about sex. Her mother would have done that, he comforted himself, forgetting that his wife had died when Tracy was thirteen. And surely they had discussed such matters at that advanced school of hers, he thought bracingly. Tracy didn't need his advice.

Such matters had been discussed at Tracy's school, but not in the classroom. The girls had pooled their ignorance and consequently Tracy half knew some things and misunderstood others. The result was she stood waiting for her bridegroom in a state of near terror. She did not go near the bed but stood close to the window, as if looking for a way to escape.

The family apartment at Thorn Manor consisted of two bedrooms, with attendant dressing rooms, connected by a sitting room. Each bedroom had two doors; one led to the hall and the other to the connecting sitting room. It was through the latter door of Tracy's room that the Duke finally came, dressed in a wide-lapelled, simple but very expensive-looking dressing gown. Tracy didn't move when he came in but stood rigid like a deer at bay.

It did not take the Duke long to assess the situation. "*Ma mie*," he said, his voice full of warm sympathy and just a hint of amusement, "there is no need to look like that. I am not going to eat you, I promise."

Tracy was not afraid that he would eat her; it was other unspecified things that she feared. He crossed the room to her, slowly and steadily, as one would approach a wild creature one was hoping to tame. She was trembling a little, he could see as he got closer, and her eyes were like emeralds. He made no attempt to touch her but held out a hand. "Come here to me and let us talk a little about these fears of yours."

Talking was about the only thing Tracy felt prepared to do with him at this point, and, tentatively, she took two steps forward. He put his arm lightly around her and guided her to the small settee that stood before the chimney piece. They sat down side by side and he kept his arm around her so that she was leaning against his side. "Has no one spoken to you about what takes place between a man and a woman when they are married?"

Tracy shook her head, and he reflected for a moment on the flaws of a culture that allowed young girls to come to their marriage beds in such ignorance. The Duke himself was not used to dealing with frightened virgins; his previous partners had all been women of the world, *femmes du monde* who knew very well what they were about. But he had seen fear before, on the battlefield, and he had recognized the seriousness of Tracy's state almost instantly. It was not a state he was inclined to take lightly.

Tracy sat stiffly against him, nervous under his touch, apprehensive because of his nearness. Slowly, reflectively, he began to talk. He said nothing to her of her "duty." He spoke instead of love, of how a man and a woman were but two halves of one whole, of how in marriage the halves came together and were completed. Tracy listened, conscious of his body pressed against hers, conscious of the warm hand that was slowly caressing her bare shoulder, conscious of the quiet, reassuring voice so close to her ear. As she rested there, the power his closeness had always exerted on her began to reassert itself. He was being very patient with her, she thought. The terrible strangeness, the fear of the unknown, began to recede, overcome by the magic of her husband's nearness, the tender reassurance she heard in his voice. She began to feel that she had been behaving badly. She still did not quite understand what would happen in the next half hour or so, but clearly it was foolish of her to be afraid. He stopped talking and just sat quietly, holding her.

"Adrian?" said Tracy, after a minute.

"Yes, *ma mie?*"

"I'm being awfully silly. I'm sorry."

He rubbed his cheek gently against the top of her head. "You are being silly if you think that I would ever harm you." He cradled the warm, relaxed weight of her. "Come over to the bed with me now, Tracy," he said softly.

She nodded and let him pull her up. With his arm still about her she walked across to the bed, kicked off her slippers and in a swift, graceful movement, lay down on the bed. He took off his dressing gown and lay down beside her.

He was a consummately skilled lover and he used his skill to woo his young wife. He went very slowly, very gently, and Tracy, trusting him, soon began to respond. She had never dreamed that a man's touch could make her feel the things that she was feeling. She slid her own hands over his back, feeling for herself the strength of the muscles that had so surprised her the day in the woods when he had moved the tree branch. She felt the most incredible aching tension deep within her and arched up against him, seeking release.

"Tracy," he murmured, his mouth against the beautiful curve of her throat, "this may hurt you a little." Then he came into her.

Tracy's eyes opened wide with shock. All the delightful aching tension was gone and in its place was a fierce burning pain. She tried to push him away but he held her with unbreakable strength and would not let her go. Tears of pain came unbidden to her eyes and slid down her cheeks.

"Adrian!" she said in protest. "You're hurting me!"

When he finally let her go, he raised himself on an elbow and looked down at her face. For the first time he saw the tears. "My poor darling," he said in surprise and apology. "Did I hurt you so badly?"

Tracy bit her lip. "Yes."

He kissed the tears off her cheek. "It was because it was the first time for you. It won't hurt like that again. I'm sorry."

Tracy was reflecting on his words and remembering how he had made her feel earlier when she happened to glance down. She sat up abruptly and yelped in horror. "I'm bleeding!"

At the expression on her face her husband began to laugh. When she turned large, reproachful eyes on him, he schooled his face to gravity. "That, my love, is the proof of your virginity," he said.

"Oh." She frowned thoughtfully. "It happens to everyone?"

"I have had no prior experience, but so I understand," he replied gravely.

She shot him a look and then regarded the evidence. "What a mess."

"It is indeed. You were a virgin with a vengeance," he said cordially and Tracy chuckled.

"What a delightful sound," he said, entranced. "Do it again."

"Do what again?"

"That little laugh you just gave."

Tracy frowned suspiciously. "Adrian, I think you're trying to distract me. You've ruined a perfectly beautiful nightdress. And the sheets are disgusting."

"Do you always dwell with such tenacity on the more unpleasant things of life?"

"I do when they pertain to me," Tracy said decidedly.

He sighed and lay back on the pillow, folding his hands behind his head. It was Tracy's turn now to prop herself up on her elbow. She looked down into his face and smiled slightly. "The first part was lovely," she said softly and, bending, kissed him lightly on the lips.

He didn't answer for a minute, just lay regarding her out of eyes of midnight blue. Tracy felt something vibrate in the air between them, then he smiled and it was gone. "It will all be lovely the next time, I promise," he said lightly. "And now I suggest you ring for your maid and have her change the sheets and get you a new nightdress."

"The maid? Oh dear, I'll be so horribly embarrassed."

"By the maid?" The Duke clearly thought she was being absurd. He swung himself out of bed and belted his dressing gown around him. "I'll see you in the morning," he said and bent to kiss her cheek. Tracy watched him depart through the connecting door back to his own room and felt a brief flicker of annoyance at being the one left to face the maid with the mess. For Tracy, who still called the servants the help, a maid was irrevocably a person like herself, not a faceless, depersonalized convenience. She truly would be horribly embarrassed.

The maid, however, was silent and mercifully swift. Soon Tracy, clad in a fresh white nightdress, was lying between clean new sheets. As she drifted off to sleep she spared a thought of pity for all the poor hapless girls who were unlucky enough to marry men without the kindness, tenderness and wisdom of her own husband.

Chapter 9

Gentle thou art, and therefore to be won,
Beauteous thou art, therefore to be assailed.
                                    —Shakespeare

Tracy slept deeply and woke to find the sun pouring in the window. She stretched comfortably, hopped out of bed and went to the window. As she looked out at the sun-drenched morning she saw a horse and rider come out of the woods in the distance and start up a path that led toward the house. She smiled with pleasure: the man and the swiftly moving horse seemed almost a part of each other and certainly a part of the beautiful morning. As he neared the house, the man pulled the horse up to a sedate trot and for the first time Tracy realized that the rider was her husband.

The maid came into the room behind her, and Tracy turned reluctantly from the window. "Shall I bring your breakfast up to you, Your Grace?" the girl asked.

Tracy shook her head. "I shall never get used to being addressed in such a ridiculous fashion," she said.

The maid, who was young and pretty, looked distressed. "Did I say something wrong, Your Grace? If I did, I did not mean to. I beg your pardon."

Tracy was surprised. She was used to Americans who thought of themselves as conferring a favor upon their employers by agreeing to 'help out' and who certainly would not apologize for a totally unintended error. "I only meant that I am not used to titles of nobility. 'Your Grace' sounds very strange to my American ears," she explained.

"Oh, I see." The girl looked bewildered. "Shall I bring your breakfast, then, Your Grace?"

Tracy gave it up. "No, thank you—what is your name?"

"Emma, Your Grace."

"No, thank you, Emma. I think I will dress and breakfast with the Duke. Or has he eaten already?"

"No, Your Grace."

Tracy's face brightened as an idea struck her. "Would it be too much trouble to have breakfast brought up to the sitting room?"

Emma blinked. She had had no previous experience with duchesses, but she was quite sure they did not ask their servants if anything would be "too much trouble." "Of course not, Your Grace," she said now.

"Good." Tracy looked around the room. "Who unpacked for me yesterday? Where did my yellow morning dress get stowed?" Tracy had a deplorable habit of using nautical expressions in decidedly nonnautical situations.

"I unpacked for you, Your Grace," Emma said faintly. "Mrs. Map only sent me and Robert and

Nancy and, of course, Alphonse from the Castle. Mr. and Mrs. Allen are the caretakers here, but they of course won't serve you."

"Who is Mrs. Map?" asked Tracy.

"Mrs. Map is the housekeeper at Steyning Castle, Your Grace," said Emma. "She said you would have your own personal maid with you, but, as you didn't, I . . ." Emma stopped abruptly, afraid she sounded like she was criticizing.

Tracy smiled engagingly. "I foresee that I am going to prove a sad disappointment to Mrs. Map, Emma. I don't have a personal maid. In fact, I've never had a personal maid. What on earth does a personal maid do for one?"

Emma found herself smiling back. She had never met a member of the Quality who was at all like the Duchess. "Why, a personal maid looks after your clothes and your jewels, Your Grace, and does your hair, and helps you dress . . ."

"I see." Tracy looked thoughtful. "Do all ladies—duchesses and countesses and so forth—have personal maids?"

"Yes, Your Grace." Emma had been in service for several years and she was certain of that.

"I'll tell you what, Emma, would you like to be my personal maid?" As the girl stared at her, stunned, Tracy went on, "You don't have to if you'd rather not, of course. You may very well prefer your present position." To be a lady's maid was just about the summit of any girl-in-service's ambition, Emma hastened to explain.

"It's not that I don't want the position, Your Grace. In fact, I'd love it," she said in a candid rush. "It is just that I've no training for it. I wouldn't suit you, I'm sure."

"I think you'll suit me just fine," Tracy said decidedly. "To be honest, you probably won't have a whole lot to do. You can look after my clothes, I guess, and help me with buttons and so forth." Tracy wrinkled her nose. "You don't seem to be a fussy sort of person. I can't stand people fussing over me."

"I will remember that, Your Grace. Thank you, Your Grace. Your yellow dress is hanging in the wardrobe in the dressing room, Your Grace. Shall I get it for you?"

"Yes, please. And then you can go see about breakfast."

"Yes, Your Grace," said Emma, and Tracy made a comical face behind the girl's back as she went into the alcove off the bedroom that was designated the dressing room.

When the Duke arrived back at the house after his morning ride, he was informed by Robert that breakfast was being served upstairs in the family sitting room and that the Duchess was waiting for him. The Duke washed up and entered the sitting room to find his wife looking like a ray of sunshine in a lemon-yellow morning dress, sipping coffee and looking at the paper. She looked up as the door opened and gave him a flash of very white teeth. "Good morning, Your Grace. How are you, Your Grace? I hope Your Grace enjoyed your ride. What would Your Grace like for breakfast? I told the help We Graces would like to breakfast in the sitting room. Isn't it lovely and sunny? Your Grace."

The Duke laughed and, sitting down opposite her, said, "What was that all about? Your Grace."

Tracy's eyes were brilliant with mirth. "Adrian, the girl who came to help me dress this morning called me 'Your Grace' at least ten times—in five minutes! I couldn't believe it."

He accepted a cup of coffee from her and helped himself to grilled kidneys and bacon. "You will have to get used to it, I fear. It is a term of address you will hear with some regularity from now on."

Tracy snorted. It was not a genteel, ladylike sound and her husband put down his cup and stared at her. "What was that?" he asked.

"That was a snort," she said sweetly. "A good, solid, healthy American snort. It manages to convey disbelief, derision and amusement all at the same time."

His eyes narrowed a little. "Does it, indeed?"

"Yes. Oh, and I understand from Emma—she is the girl I was telling you about—that I shall be expected to have a personal maid."

"Most certainly you should have your own maid."

"Well, I expect Emma can do the job for me. I've no idea what I ought to pay her, though."

He looked thoughtful. "I can't tell you, I'm afraid. I know what I pay my valet, but the two may not be comparable. I suggest you ask Aunt Georgina when we return to London."

She nodded. "Good idea. Oh, they sent the papers up with breakfast. Do you want the *Post*?"

"Yes, please." He took the paper from her and silence descended as they made their way through the coffee and a plate of buttered muffins.

"What would you like to do today?" he asked finally, folding his paper and smiling at her across the table.

"I would love to see some of the countryside," she replied promptly. "It looks such a lovely day."

"It is. I had the phaeton brought down. Shall we take that?"

"Oh, yes. I don't want to be cooped up inside a carriage on a day like this." She gave him a slanting look from under lowered lids. "Did your brother tell you my disgraceful secret?"

He frowned a little and then as her meaning struck him he looked amused. "Do you mean the fact that you don't ride?"

"Yes."

"Don't let it worry you," he said easily. "It is not important."

She remembered the vision she had had of him that morning. "I should like to learn," she said tentatively. "I'm not afraid, you know. I just never had the opportunity."

Her husband grinned. "So Harry told me. He also said you could sail anything that floats."

"Well . . ." Her wide mouth quirked up a little at the corners. "Maybe not *anything* . . ." He laughed.

They had a lovely day together. It could have been extremely awkward; they were two people who hardly knew each other and they were thrown almost entirely into each other's company with little distraction in the form of other people. But it was not awkward. They had a long and leisurely drive about the estate and the neighborhood. Tracy was interested in everything and noticed everything. Most of all, she noticed people. "What a marvelous-looking old man," she said at one point, as they drove past a man working in a field. The man had turned toward the road when he heard the horses and had taken off his hat in respect as they went by. The Duke had nodded at him graciously and Tracy had smiled, but only one of them had really seen him.

They had passed a group of children playing in the front yard of a cottage and Tracy had given them a friendly wave. "Did you notice that dark-eyed little boy?" she asked the Duke. "What a beautiful child!" He had noticed the children in the mass but not as individuals. He looked at his wife with interest. It seemed remarkable to him that she should be so observant.

In the afternoon the Duke had taken out a gun and Tracy had settled down to read in the garden. He was surprised, and pleased, by her independence. He had not expected to be able to get off by himself. "I would just love to sit in the sunshine and read," she had said, half apologetically. "Unless, of course, there is something you want me to do?"

He had replied that she must do whatever she wished to do and that he would be very happy to go out with a gun for a few hours. She was still reading when he returned and, instead of going directly into the house, he detoured to the garden. She was so absorbed she did not hear him coming and it wasn't until he spoke her name that she looked up.

"Oh, Adrian!" She looked at his shooting jacket,

gun and the leather pouch he carried. "Are you back so soon?"

"It is after five o'clock," he said.

"Is it? Good heavens, I had no idea it was so late. I have been reading a new novel called *Persuasion* by Miss Austen," she explained. "It is marvelous."

"I don't believe I've ever read anything by Miss Austen," he said.

"She is a genius," Tracy said enthusiastically. "And hilariously funny as well, although this book is a little different from her previous novels."

"Do you read a great deal, Tracy?"

"Constantly, I'm afraid. I brought six books with me to Thorn Manor."

He threw back his head and shouted with laughter. When he had got his breath back, he said, "Promise me solemnly, *ma mie*, that you won't reveal that fact to a soul. Think of my reputation! My wife found it necessary to bring along six books on her honeymoon. I should never live it down."

Tracy had been regarding his mirth with good-humored bewilderment, but now her own rich laugh rippled out. "I hadn't thought of it that way." She gave him an impish look. "It will be our secret."

"Thank you, darling," he said fervently. "Do you think you could tear yourself away from your book for long enough to have dinner?"

"Certainly," she replied and, rising, accompanied him to the house, chatting companionably all the while.

Chapter 10

Lord of my love, to whom in vassalage
Thy merit hath my duty strongly knit.
                                    —Shakespeare

Alphonse, the Duke's chef who had been sent up
from the Castle, outdid himself at dinner. Tracy,
who was a very good cook herself, was deeply
impressed. The food she had had on her visit to
Steyning Castle and the last evening's meal as well
had been superlative, but on those occasions her
mind had been too distracted to allow her to appre-
ciate it as it deserved to be appreciated.

"Is Alphonse French?" she asked the Duke, reverently regarding a morsel of squab before she put
it into her mouth.

"Yes. I brought him from Paris with me when I
came home last winter. I had to bribe him shame-
lessly, but he was worth it."

"He certainly was," said Tracy, mentally planning to see if she could extract some of the chef's
secrets from him.

After dinner they went into the library and the

Duke proposed a game of chess. Tracy looked at him measuringly. "Only if you give me a handicap," she said at last.

He looked disappointed. "I did not know you were so poor spirited."

"I don't mind losing, but I hate to lose badly," Tracy said frankly. "You may be the image of a British gentleman, but I'll bet you're a killer. Give me a queen and a rook."

"A queen and a rook!"

"Tsk, tsk, Adrian. I didn't know you were so poor spirited."

"I hate to lose, period," he said ruefully and Tracy smiled triumphantly.

"I knew it."

He looked at her, dark blue eyes narrowed. "All right. A queen and a rook."

Silence descended as they bent over the chess board. Tracy was quite a good player, but the Duke excelled. Without the handicap she would not have had a chance. As it was, the game was very nearly even as they came down toward the end with the edge going to Tracy as she had both her knights and he had only one. She had lost her queen a few moves before.

She stared at the board intently. "I should win this," she muttered. "I'm ahead." She moved a knight and next move lost her rook. It didn't take the Duke long to checkmate her. "Damn," said Tracy disgustedly.

"Shame on you, *ma mie*," he said. "You should have put up a better end game than that."

"I know. I never play a decent end game. I do

fine until I have to finish it off. I just can't seem to figure out how to go about it. I dither."

He was smiling at her. "You don't have the killer instinct." His voice was softly amused.

"I guess not."

He reached out and covered her hand with his. "I shouldn't at all like a wife who had the killer instinct." Her eyelids dropped a little in a kind of acknowledgment.

The tea tray came in and after, the Duke said, "You go along to bed, Tracy. *I* am going to read for a bit. I'll see you in the morning." Her eyebrows raised a little in surprise and he said levelly, "I am going to be very noble tonight. I don't want to hurt you again. Let's give it another day."

"Oh." She looked at him for a moment, her eyes serious, then she smiled. "So noble a noble," she said mockingly, blew him a kiss, turned her beautiful back and left.

The following day they went fishing. There was a small but secluded lake on the Thorn Manor estate, and the Duke had told her that it was well stocked with fish. To Tracy's mind, nothing equaled saltwater fishing, but the lake had looked inviting and freshwater fishing was better than no fishing at all. They left the house in the afternoon, and it was warm and sunny when they arrived at the smooth, clear expanse of water that was Thorn Lake.

Tracy was dressed in a blue cotton shirt-dress and thin blue leather slippers. She took her fishing rod from the Duke, put it down on the grass and proceeded to roll up the sleeves of her dress. She then took her shoes off. "Ah, the grass feels wonderful," she said, and he noticed that her feet were bare. She baited her hook with professional detachment and looked at him expectantly.

His blue eyes glinted at her. "Go ahead," he said. "I'll move off onto the rocks over there."

She nodded and expertly cast her line into the water. He did not move immediately but stood regarding her. He was, as his aunt had often remarked, a very fastidious man, and the sight of his wife barefoot and dressed in a plain cotton dress with the sleeves rolled up ought not to have appealed to him at all. But it did. For one thing, Tracy didn't look even remotely disheveled. She could have spent hours rolling her sleeves in just that way, arranging her collar in just that way, so perfect did they look on her. She had a way with clothes, he reflected, that was more French than English. Whatever she wore, it looked marvelous. It was the way she wore it—as if, under the circumstances, it was impossible for anyone to wear anything else. She began to pull in her line and he moved over to the rocks he had pointed out and began to fish himself.

They had quite a successful afternoon and the Duke's bucket was respectably full when he decided to call a halt. Tracy had stopped fishing about fifteen minutes before and was lying back on the grass, sleepy from the sun, her eyes closed, her hands behind her head. He put the fishing gear into the phaeton and sat down beside her. Her lashes, a darker brown than her hair, lay on her cheeks. Her skin was honey colored, not the white-white of an Englishwoman's. Damp brown-blonde curls clus-

"You must be part mermaid," he answered and, bending, picked up one of the towels.

"No, I'm just a girl from Massachusetts." She smiled and reached for the towel he held. But he shook his head and proceeded to dry her himself, after which he laid her down in the shelter of two old trees and made love to her.

That was the afternoon of their last day at Thorn Manor. When they returned to the house, Tracy was met by a very upset Emma. "Oh, Your Grace! Alphonse fell down this afternoon and hit his head and the doctor has been and says he must stay in bed for at least two days!"

"Good heavens." Tracy had hardly walked in the door; the Duke had taken the horses around to the stables. "However did he come to fall?"

"There was a wet spot on the kitchen floor. He hit his head on the table."

"Is he all right?" Tracy asked with swift concern. "The doctor didn't think it was serious?"

"No, Your Grace. A concussion, he said."

"Well, that's all right then."

"But, Your Grace," Emma almost wailed, "I don't know who is to cook your dinner for you. Mrs. Allen boils everything, she says. And I can cook eggs and fry bread, but I don't think His Grace . . ."

The corners of Tracy's mouth indented. "No," she said, "a boiled dinner or eggs certainly will not do for His Grace. I suppose it's too late to find someone else?"

"Mrs. Allen doesn't have any suggestions."

"Well, don't get into such a pucker, Emma. I guess I'll just have to cook dinner myself?"

"*You*, Your Grace?"

Tracy laughed. "Me. Before I became a duchess, I was just an American girl, Emma, and American girls learn to cook. I'll just have a look in the kitchen to see what's available, and then I should very much like to wash my hair."

So it was that on the last evening of her honeymoon, Tracy ate a dinner she had cooked herself. So did the servants, for whom she had done a roast beef, refusing to allow them to dine on the eggs that would otherwise have been their fate.

The Duke had had no idea that his wife was in the kitchen until she arrived in the drawing room clad in an apron that she proceeded to remove and place on the back of a chair as she announced with aplomb, "Dinner is served."

There was a lovely clear soup, fillets of the fish they had caught that afternoon served in herb butter, and tender, succulent chicken. Emma, who had had strict instructions on when to turn things over and when to take them off the heat, was in charge in the kitchen. Robert, serving, couldn't help but look with amazement at the Duchess, who sat serenely eating her food and sipping her wine, giving no sign at all that she had been chopping vegetables in the kitchen an hour ago.

The Duke was scarcely less amazed. "Did you actually cook this?" he asked as he tasted the delicious fish.

"I did," said Tracy. "My mother was an excellent cook—although not in the same category as Alphonse. She taught me to cook when I was still a little girl."

"But did you cook in America?" Clearly he couldn't quite understand how his wife had come to acquire her skill.

"We had a cook, of course, but either Mother or I took over on her day off. And we often did the baking." Tracy smiled at his expression. "It is not that easy to find help in America, Adrian. Most good households only have three or four people. There is nothing like the number of people you have working for you in England. Except in the South, and that is only because of slavery, a situation we all disapprove of deeply."

"Except, of course, the Southerners," he said.

"Not really. Most slaveowners don't defend the institution, you know. The problem is how to get rid of it. But they will. It has only been a few years since the Northern states emancipated their slaves. England has only outlawed slavery quite recently also. One after the other the Southern states will follow suit, I'm sure."

"Even with the plantations requiring so many people to work them?"

"About a year ago a group of plantation owners and slaveholders formed the American Colonization Society. Its president is Bushrod Washington, President Washington's nephew and the owner of Mount Vernon. They want to try to repatriate the Blacks back to Africa. Most of the members are slaveholders who want to find a practicable way of accomplishing emancipation. So you see, progress is being made. It is all a question of time."

"Well, that is certainly encouraging," he remarked and changed the subject.

That night, Tracy lay awake in her husband's arms, listening to the night sounds coming from outside the open window and wishing they did not have to leave tomorrow. She knew that these last five days with Adrian were a unique, never-to-be-repeated time; they were days that were almost out of time, isolated, idyllic, spellbound. They would go back to London and pick up their real life, go back to being people who existed in the context of a world that included other people, other demands, other responsibilities. It was inevitable that they do so, yet Tracy wished now that it did not have to come so soon. She sighed softly and her husband stirred. "Is anything wrong, *ma mie?*"

"No." She smiled a little in the darkness and he could hear the smile in her voice. "I was just thinking that our honeymoon has been too short. I only finished one book, you know." She turned her head so that her lips were against his bare chest. "I don't believe any girl ever had a honeymoon more wonderful than mine," she murmured.

He didn't answer, but in half a minute he had turned her over and come into her. She was startled and opened her mouth to protest, but his own mouth came down over hers, crushing the words. He made no attempt to caress her and the hands holding her shoulders were hard and inescapable. After a moment, Tracy's mouth answered to his and she arched up against him, shuddering with passion.

After, she lay nestled against him, relaxed and sleepy. "That was incredible," she murmured.

Gently he kissed her temple. "Go to sleep," he said, his voice like a caress. "Go to sleep, my love." And she did.

Chapter 11

This thou perceivest, which makes thy love
  more strong,
To love that well which thou must leave ere
  long.
                     —Shakespeare

Tracy was very silent during the drive back to
London and the Duke made little attempt to draw
her into conversation. When they reached the out-
skirts of the city he asked her if she wanted to stop
first at the Clarendon to see her father, and she said
that she did.

She had pushed her father to the bottom of her
mind for the last week, but now reality was avoida-
ble no longer. She would see him today. And for a
few more days. Then he would go back to America and she would never see him again. When they
reached the hotel her husband said tactfully, "You
go up first, *ma mie.* I'll come along in a bit." She
smiled a little tremulously, nodded and left him to
go upstairs.

His daughter had been very much in Mr. Bodmin's mind for the last week. When he had seen her drive off with the Duke he had been attacked by feelings of uneasiness and guilt. He knew he had been instrumental in bringing about this marriage. He had been sure he was doing the right thing. However, as he watched Tracy drive off in the impressive ducal carriage, his certainty had wavered. What had he done, trusting his girl to this unknown young man?

So he searched her face carefully when she came into his suite, looking for evidence of happiness or pain. His first impression, as she blew into his drawing room like a fresh breeze, was that she glowed. But there was a shade of anxiety in her eyes, he thought, as she chatted with him easily and amusingly. He was not to know that the anxiety was for himself, that he seemed smaller to her, and grayer, and far too thin.

Then the Duke was at the door and Tracy turned her face to him for a minute before looking back to her father. The young couple stayed for perhaps twenty more minutes, and by the time they left, Mr. Bodmin was quite certain that everything was all right indeed.

The next day, Mr. Bodmin called at the Duke's town house in Berkeley Square and asked to see his son-in-law alone. The Duke took him into the library and offered him some Madeira, which the American accepted and sipped appreciatively.

"I want to talk business with you, Adrian," Mr. Bodmin began purposefully.

The Duke was a little startled. He thought all that had been taken care of by the lawyers. But he nodded courteously and said, "Certainly, sir. What do you wish to say to me?"

"It may seem strange to you that I did not tell you this before, but I wanted to wait until after your marriage. To be blunt, I wanted to satisfy myself that you could make Tracy happy."

"I see." The Duke's voice was cool. "And are you satisfied?"

"Yes. There is a certain look in a woman's eyes when she . . ." Mr. Bodmin broke off and the two men looked at each other in perfect comprehension. Then the older man said simply, "I am a dying man, Adrian."

The Duke's blue eyes darkened. "What?"

"Yes. It's my lungs. I'm done for, I'm afraid."

"Does Tracy know?"

"No. And I don't want her to know. Not until she has to. It shouldn't take too long."

The Duke looked at his father-in-law for a minute, then said softly, "You are a brave man, sir."

Those words, coming from his son-in-law, meant something. Mr. Bodmin raised his hand a little, then said prosaically, "I am going home to settle my estate. I shall sell my ships; I know several people who will be interested. I should realize millions, Adrian, and it will all come to you."

"It will come to Tracy," said the Duke quietly.

Mr. Bodmin shrugged. "It's the same thing, isn't it, under English law?"

The Duke frowned. "I don't want your money, sir. The arrangements we made previous to our marriage were quite generous enough. Tie the money up in a trust for Tracy."

"Do you mean that?"

"Yes." The Duke's voice was pleasant but adamant.

"I guess I could do that."

"Certainly you could." The Duke looked steadily at his father-in-law and said directly, "You needn't worry about Tracy, sir. I shall take very good care of her, I promise you."

"Thank you, my boy. That is all that is important to me, really." Mr. Bodmin put down his glass. "I'll settle the money on Tracy, then, and on your children."

The Duke smiled faintly. "Thank you, sir."

"Well then, I think I'll see if Tracy would like to take a drive with me."

"She is in the morning parlor, I believe," the Duke said quietly. The two men looked at each other for a moment, and then Mr. Bodmin nodded and left.

All the Duke could do for his father-in-law at present was to allow him the comfort of his daughter's company as much as possible, and this he did, withdrawing from the scene with beautiful ease and tact. The couple made just one appearance at a large social function, a ball given by Lady Maria Egerton. The rest of the week consisted of small family parties, from which the Duke contrived to be frequently absent.

Mr. Bodmin had accompanied them to the Egerton ball and had derived enormous satisfaction from it. When the major domo had announced: "His Grace the Duke of Hastings and Her Grace the Duchess," he had felt as if the crowning achievement of his life had been realized.

Tracy had looked beautiful, and she had been a center of flattering attention all evening. As the Duchess of Hastings she was still as gracefully and naturally charming as she had been before her elevation to her present exalted rank. It would be impossible, Mr. Bodmin thought complacently, for anyone to resist the radiant warmth of his Tracy.

And nothing gave Mr. Bodmin more pleasure than to see his son-in-law in society. There was an air about Adrian that was difficult to define but not at all difficult to distinguish. He was not haughty or arrogant, yet one never had any doubt when in his company that one was in the presence of someone who stood very high in the world. A *grand seigneur*, Tracy had called him. There was such serenity about him, the large and beautiful ease of a man who had always been certain of himself and of his position. He never made demands. He never said or did anything that indicated he thought himself superior. But, instinctively, he was deferred to. Mr. Bodmin did not think it was just his rank that commanded such respect; it was something in himself. He was the real thing, the genuine article; when Mr. Bodmin had acquired the Duke for his daughter he had gotten value.

Tracy had known her father would enjoy seeing her appear publicly as the Duchess of Hastings, and she had determined to give him a good show. She was finding it increasingly difficult to maintain her fictional ignorance of his condition, and she both looked forward to and dreaded his imminent departure. She did not know if Adrian was aware of his

condition. She thought, from the way he arranged
that father and daughter be alone together, that he
was. But she couldn't speak of it. Not yet.

The day finally dawned for Mr. Bodmin's departure. He was leaving early in the morning to drive
to Dover where his ship was waiting, so his dinner
at Berkeley Square with his daughter and son-in-
law was to be his farewell.

Tracy got through the dinner largely because of
the Duke. It was his genius for charm that buoyed
up father and daughter and cast a glow of warmth
and cheerfulness that the two were scarcely feeling.
Because of him it was almost possible to believe
that they were parting only temporarily, that many
good times lay ahead in the future.

When it came time for her father to leave, Tracy
kissed him warmly, smiled brilliantly and said,
"Now you be sure to come back to England soon,
Papa. I'll miss you, you know."

Mr. Bodmin held her closely for a minute. "I'll
miss you too, honey. But it will make me happy
just to think of you."

He then shook hands with his son-in-law who
said, "I'll see you out to the carriage, sir."

When the Duke came back into the house the
hall was empty. He looked in the drawing room but
finding that empty as well proceeded to the library.
There he found Tracy, standing looking down at a
great globe. "Is he gone?" she asked.

"Yes." He crossed to her, but she continued to
look down at the globe, spinning it slowly. Her
face was expressionless. "You know, don't you?" he
asked softly.

She turned and he took her in his arms. "Oh, Adrian," was all she could say.

After a minute he said, "Come and sit down. I'm going to get you a brandy." When it was in her hands, she looked at it blankly. "Drink it, Tracy," he said firmly, and she obeyed him.

"Did he tell you?" she asked, after she had finished it and the warmth was flowing through her chilled veins.

"Yes. The day after we returned from Hertfordshire. He didn't think you knew."

"I overheard him tell Mr. Rush one afternoon in London. He said he didn't want me to know. He didn't want me to see him as—less than he was." Her voice trembled. "He is such a proud man."

"And so you decided to pretend ignorance."

"It was what he wanted. *I* wanted to be with him, to take care of him; but it seemed to me that the greatest comfort I could give him was my supposed ignorance."

"I see," he said slowly.

"But oh, Adrian, to let him go like this . . ." At last the tears began to slide down her face.

He remembered her brilliant smile. "You were splendid, *ma mie*. And you were right to do as you did. It gave him happiness to think he was sparing you."

She was sobbing in his arms now. "But it wasn't fair," she got out.

"No," he replied soberly, softly stroking her hair. "It wasn't fair."

After a while her sobs slowed and then ceased, but she made no attempt to move away from him.

Adrian was all she had now, she thought somewhat incoherently. She wasn't going to let go of him.

At length he got her on her feet and up the stairs to her bedroom. He undressed her and slowly, gently, comfortingly, made love to her until she fell asleep.

Chapter 12

I say, therefore, that since the nature of man in youthful age is so much inclined to sense, it may be granted the courtier, while he is young, to love sensually;

—*The Book of the Courtier*

For the present the Duke and Duchess of Hastings remained in London. The Season was still in full swing; town would not begin to empty until August and the Duke exerted gentle pressure on his wife to remain. Tracy was not in the mood for parties, but Adrian felt she would be better off keeping busy. He did not want to give her too much time to brood about her father.

He was anxious to remain in London for his own sake as well. It was time, he thought, for him to take up the threads of his own life again. Ever since he had returned from France he had been occupied with family business: first sorting out his father's financial debacle and then getting married to rectify the catastrophic position he had found himself in. Thanks to Mr. Bodmin's very generous settlement, his financial problems had largely been solved. It would be the work of some years to see his estates restored to what they once had been, but the crushing load of debt had been lifted. For the first time since he had come home, he had no money worries. Finally he could turn his attention to what really interested him.

What interested the Duke was foreign affairs. For years in France he had worked with the Ambassadorial Conference and the Duke of Wellington had found his assistance invaluable. The Duke knew all the important European diplomats and, what was even more important, he had their confidence. Viscount Castlereagh, the Foreign Secretary, was anxious to annex his assistance for the Foreign Office. In the young Duke, Lord Castlereagh had discovered someone whose world view matched the Secretary's own. The Duke thought in terms of Europe; nearly everyone else in England thought only in terms of their own small island. Castlereagh had been single-handedly running his country's foreign affairs for years and he was getting tired. In the Duke of Hastings he recognized a possible successor; and he was very willing to share some of the burdens of his office.

The Duke's smooth entrance into the political scene surprised few of the seasoned European diplomats. It was more surprising to the British, who had, with their usual insularity, paid little attention to European affairs since the close of the war. The Duke had not been in London for a month before it became clear to all interested observers that in regard to foreign affairs there were now three men who counted in Britain: Lord Castlereagh, the Duke of Wellington and the Duke of Hastings.

It took Tracy longer than most to recognize her husband's position. It was many weeks before she succeeded in seeing him as anything but Adrian, her husband, the man she adored.

Their physical relationship was still new and, to her, all absorbing. No matter what he might be when he was away from her, when he was with her he was her lover. The passion that had been born between them at Thorn Manor grew and deepened as the weeks passed. It seemed to Tracy that Adrian was as absorbed in her as she was in him. She remembered vividly the first time he had skillfully extricated her from a particularly glittering party at a ridiculously early hour. She had been talking to Lord Holland and someone else about the strange new novel *Frankenstein* when she felt Adrian's hand lightly touch her shoulder. After a few words with Lord Holland he expertly detached her from the two men and turned her toward the door. "Let's go home," he said softly in her ear.

She had moved with him willingly, but at his words she protested, "What will people think if we leave so early?"

He smiled with devastating charm at Lady Jersey. In a low voice he murmured to Tracy, "They will think I am taking you home to bed. And they will be right." Tracy had blushed, but she made no further protest.

It was a scene that was repeated more than once. Tracy sometimes felt as if she were walking through the world in a fog, blind to everything except one man. It astonished her—the incredible rapture of their lovemaking. He had released something in her that she had not known existed, and she found herself responding to him with an abandon she would not have thought possible a few short weeks ago. She thought sometimes of her fears on her wedding night. And she laughed.

It was only gradually that it began to impinge on Tracy's consciousness that Adrian was something more than just her husband. He was the Duke of Hastings, of course. She had always known that. She had even known that his position was bound to make demands on her, but that knowledge had somehow been buried beneath the sensuous haze of love that had enveloped her since her honeymoon.

Lady Bridgewater had sounded the alarm first. "I do not think you ought to spend so much time with Lord Holland, my dear," she said to Tracy one afternoon. They were drinking tea in the drawing room of Hastings House when she brought up the matter that was the reason for her call on her nephew's wife.

Tracy stared. "Why ever not? Isn't he respectable?"

Lady Bridgewater put down her cup. "I realize that our ways and our politics are strange to you, Tracy, but really, you must make an effort to learn. Lord Holland is perfectly respectable, but he is a Whig. Good heavens—Charles Fox was his uncle! Certainly you must be polite to him. But, politically, he is not one of ours. Do you understand?"

"I guess so," said Tracy unwillingly. "You mean, it's like the Crowinshields and the Derbys in Salem.

The Crowinshields are Republicans and they have their balls in Washington Hall while the Derbys are Federalists and hold theirs in Hamilton Hall. Only, we went to both. Papa was a Federalist once, but they kicked him out when he supported Mr. Jefferson's embargo."

She had a suspicion she wasn't making much sense, a suspicion confirmed by Lady Bridgewater's reply. "Really, Tracy," said that lady in icily composed tones. "I don't understand a word of what you are saying. Pray, what have these people got to do with Adrian, with your position as his wife?"

Tracy sighed. "Nothing, I guess," she answered glumly.

It was a phrase she was to hear with ever increasing frequency: "your position as his wife." She rebelled a little against it at first.

"Sometimes I wish I was just plain Mrs. Deincourt," she said to her husband one night when he came into her room to say goodbye. He was dining with Lord Castlereagh and she was going to the theatre with a party of Lady Bridgewater's.

He looked at his wife's slender back for a minute in silence. She was seated at her dressing table waiting for Emma to come and fasten a necklace around her throat. The Duke stepped forward, took the diamonds from the girl and said calmly, "Her Grace will not be needing you until later." Emma immediately left the room and Tracy swung around to face him, laughter in her eyes.

"Really, Adrian! How do you know when I'll be needing my maid?"

He didn't answer her but stood holding the spill

of diamonds, his gaze steady on her lovely, slightly flushed face. "You really mean that, don't you?" His voice was very serious.

"Mean what? About my maid?"

"No." He gestured impatiently and the diamonds flashed. "You really would be happier being plain Mrs. Deincourt."

"Yes," she answered a little mournfully, "I would. In fact, I remember just before we were married, when I was wondering whether or not to marry you, that I thought I would do it like a shot if you were an American. It was your being a duke that worried me." She sighed. "I don't know if I can live up to you, Adrian."

"You don't have to live up to me," he said, his voice deepening to a note she knew well. "All you have to do is be yourself." He came toward her, but it was not to put the necklace around her throat. Tracy closed her eyes as she felt his lips on her bare neck. "I wish I didn't have a dinner engagement," he murmured, and Tracy shivered.

"I know."

After a minute he raised his head and looked deeply into her eyes. She felt herself melting in a way that was all too familiar. "I won't be late," he said softly. His fingers lightly caressed her bare shoulder and then he was gone.

She had great difficulty paying attention to the play. She kept seeing a face that was very different from the ones on the stage, hearing a voice whose timbre turned her whole insides to jelly. Lady Bridgewater was annoyed by her obvious inattention and even more annoyed when she insisted on returning home immediately after the play was over.

Adrian was waiting for her. He didn't seem at all perturbed by the thought that she might have offended his aunt.

Chapter 13

That I might see what the old world could say
To this composed wonder of your frame.
                                —Shakespeare

The Duke was very pleased with his marriage, and
not solely for financial reasons. In fact, when Mr.
Bodmin had offered him a great deal more money,
he had instinctively and unhesitatingly refused. It
was a decision he did not regret making. He was
not a man who was inclined to examine his own
motives deeply; he always acted largely out of his
own beautifully refined instincts and his instinct in
this case had bade him refuse the inheritance. It had
something to do, he knew, with his feelings for
Tracy, which were very different from what he
had thought they would be.

It seemed to him part of his astonishing luck that
he had gotten such a girl for his wife. It did not
worry him anymore that she was an American; it
was part of her charm for him. He loved the
knowledge that she cared not the snap of her
lovely fingers for his titles or his possessions. Such

unconcern had seemed incredible to him at first, but he soon saw for himself that it was real.

They had been important to her father. Beneath his republican exterior there lurked the soul of an Englishman in William Bodmin. The Duke knew that Mr. Bodmin would never have allowed Tracy to marry a nobleman of whom he did not approve, but the Duke was also in no doubt that it was his ancient title and his possessions that had made him, in Tracy's father's eyes, an eligible *parti*.

But Tracy would rather be plain Mrs. Deincourt, his wife. When she had told him that, when she had said she would have married him "like a shot" if he had been an American, the Duke felt only enormous gratification. He had married the one woman in the world capable of loving him for himself alone. In his eyes his marriage had turned out to be virtually perfect. He looked to the future with the beautiful serenity of a happy man.

It was a serenity Tracy did not share. As the weeks went by and she began to surface from the submarine depths of pure passion and fix her eyes on the surface of the world, she began to feel uneasy. Much as she might desire to be "just plain Mrs. Deincourt," the fact remained that she was not; she was the Duchess of Hastings, wife of one of England's premier noblemen and rising political stars.

Her uneasiness did not stem, at least at first, from her husband. He never said or did anything that even slightly indicated he was dissatisfied with the wife he had chosen. His aunt was less sanguine. Lady Bridgewater had made several pointed remarks indicating that she thought Tracy was not living up to her newly acquired position in life.

Adrian was clearly destined to be a government minister and all the wives of government ministers were deeply involved in their husbands' careers. That fact became quite clear to Tracy during the month of August, which she and the Duke spent in London. The majority of the *ton* had deserted town for the pleasures of Brighton, but the government and the embassy personnel had remained. Tracy saw a great deal of the political elite of England without the softening addition of the purely social element, and what she saw caused her deep concern.

She brought up one of her problems to the Duke one evening toward the middle of August. They were spending a rare evening at home, both of them sitting comfortably in the drawing room with the French windows open to let in the cool air from the garden. Tracy was holding a book and Adrian was intently reading some Foreign Office papers Lord Castlereagh had given him that afternoon. She watched him for a minute in silence, quietly closed her book and said, "I never realized you were so interested in politics, Adrian." He looked up, surprise on his face, and she added, "I guess I mean I hadn't realized you were so *involved* in politics. You weren't, were you, before we were married?"

Courteously he put down his papers. "No," he replied, "I was not. But that was not because of lack of interest, *ma mie*. I had the affairs of my father's estate to attend to. Then, I was busy getting married." He sent her a charming smile. "Now that we are settled, of course I will take up the duties of government."

She sat silent for a minute, pondering that "of course." It fit in perfectly with what Lady Bridgewater had said to her yesterday. Adrian belonged to that class in English society whose blood and training decreed the business of government to be a primary duty. It was a natural thing for him to go into government, she thought now, looking at his beautiful, slightly puzzled face. To him it seemed equally as natural that a place at the top should be waiting for him. He was puzzled as to why she should find this surprising.

"I did not realize you would be a part of the government," she explained. "In America, our politics are so different. One doesn't simply go into government because of one's class." Tracy had a way of saying the word class that made it sound as if she were talking about a peculiarly noxious odor. "In my country," she concluded grandly, "one must first be elected."

"We have elections as well," he pointed out in a markedly reasonable tone. "All of the House of Commons is elected. The only difference is that we have the House of Lords and you do not."

"That is not the only difference!" she replied hotly. "The House of Commons may be elected, Adrian, but they are not elected by the people. They are elected at the whim of some great lord. The suffrage in England is limited to the moneyed class."

"Certainly it is," he agreed pleasantly. "It is the only sensible arrangement. How can one possibly give the vote to uneducated, illiterate people? It is perfectly impossible, Tracy, to trust a farsighted, passionless policy to men whose minds are unused to thought and undisciplined to study. Naturally, the government of the country is commended to men who have the tools both of intellect and wealth to undertake it successfully."

Her eyes had turned very green. "It is not like that in my country."

His eyes glinted with amusement. "Oh, yes it is, *ma mie*," he replied unexpectedly. "Who are your presidents? Men from the landowning, slaveowning 'aristocracy' of Virginia. As is quite natural. They are the men who have the leisure and the fortune to undertake the business of government."

"Are you telling me that you think the governments of our countries are the same?" she asked incredulously.

"No, of course not." He was beginning to sound a little impatient. "America is a republic. It believes, at least in theory, that 'all men are created equal.' That is not the case in England."

"I can see that."

"The reality of the matter, Tracy," he said seriously, "is that there are those who are leaders and then there are the masses who are not. However, if one is fortunate enough to be one of the former, one has a duty and a responsibility to exercise one's talents for the common good of all."

"In short, you regard yourself not as responsible *to* the people, but rather as responsible *for* them."

He smiled. "Precisely."

Tracy was looking very somber. It shook her a little to hear him voice so clearly a philosophy with which she was in complete disagreement. "But *I* don't believe that, Adrian," she said slowly, staring down at her hands clasped in her lap.

"I don't ask that you should," he returned tranquilly. "You are an American; quite naturally your political views do not coincide with mine."

"But don't you see how awkward a situation that puts me in?" she asked earnestly, raising her eyes to his face. "Lord Castlereagh is a Tory—Lady Castlereagh is a Tory; Lord Bridgewater is a Tory—Lady Bridgewater is a Tory; Lord Holland is a Whig—Lady Holland is a Whig. You are a Tory—and I am a Republican!"

"Practically a revolutionary," he said good-humoredly.

"It's not funny, Adrian! I feel as if I've got my back up against a wall."

He was suddenly very serious. "Tracy, I do not ask you to change your opinions. I do not *want* you to change your opinions. I am perfectly capable of representing what I believe in; you do not have to carry my flag." He got out of his chair and came across to the sofa on which she was seated. "*Ma mie?*" he said softly. "Do you understand what I am saying? You are not to worry about such things."

Tracy was not totally convinced by his words, but she lacked the will to resist. He had possession of both her hands and was bending toward her. She wanted to tell him that it was not quite so easy, but it was impossible to think when he was so close to her. She felt herself to be, as always, completely in his power. "Yes," she heard herself murmuring weakly. "I understand."

Adrian had only put into words things about

himself that Tracy had been noticing for a while now. One of the most disconcerting things to her about her husband was how, below the level of a certain social class, he never *saw* people. As far as he was concerned, one footman was just like another. To him they were "the masses." He was always courteous, always reasonable, but he didn't really see people who were very far below the level of his own high head.

Tracy, to the contrary, saw everyone. Democracy to her was not a political theory or a form of government. It was a way of life. Her sense of human equality was as natural to her as breathing. She found the class-consciousness of the English profoundly disturbing. It disturbed her most of all that her husband so obviously represented all of its blindest beliefs.

And yet—much of what was fine in Adrian sprang from his feelings about aristocracy. And, to be honest, much of what fascinated her in him sprang from it as well. He *was* a duke. It was an inseparable part of him. She had thought, once, that she would be happier marrying him if he were an American. But as the weeks went by she realized that the very idea of Adrian as an American was ludicrous. If he were an American, he would not be Adrian.

She loved him passionately and she found, a little to her own surprise, that she was coming to admire him as well. He was, in so many ways, completely admirable. Aside from his extraordinary personal charm, he had intelligence and seriousness. As a good American she had always believed that ability, not birth, was the measure of a man. It appeared that her husband had both.

She was going to be the wife of a government minister and she decided that she would have to put her shoulder to the wheel and do her best for him. She could not change her politics, but whatever else was necessary she would do. Or die trying.

She would be expected to entertain for him. That was one thing that became clear to her as she attended dinner after dinner, reception after reception. Parliament was not in session, but the government had remained in town to try to deal with the country's economic crises. The August dinners and receptions were a great deal smaller than the huge crushes of the July Season, but there were there great men and beautiful women. The wives and daughters of some of England's highest nobles were her hostesses. The important role of these women pressed in on her from all sides as the weeks went by.

She took Adrian's advice and announced her own political creed at a dinner party at Bridgewater House. She was standing in a wide group of people before the fireplace waiting to go into dinner and politics were being discussed, as usual. Mr. Park, who was at the Treasury Board, turned to her. "What would you do, Duchess, if you were in Parliament?" he asked.

It was the sort of question she would previously have turned aside with a laugh and a comment about her ignorance. Tonight she took a deep breath, sent a dazzling smile around the group and answered him. "If I were in Parliament, Mr. Park, I should vote for every reform that could possibly be voted for. I should be for universal manhood suffrage, workers' rights, tenants' rights, the education of everybody, and the abolition of the House of Lords."

When Tracy had smiled all the men in the group had imperceptibly leaned toward her. When she finished speaking they were all still staring with pleasure at her lovely, animated face. Lord Liverpool, the Prime Minister and a very stiff Tory, said to her husband, "You've married a regular revolutionary, Hastings."

Adrian smiled. "Yes, but I knew that before the fact, so I can't complain."

"Certainly not," said Lord Liverpool, looking at Tracy with open admiration, and all of the gentlemen smiled in agreement.

Nobody seemed to be at all disturbed by her radical stand. As the evening went on, she realized it was because they simply did not take her seriously. She was an American. They didn't expect her to be sensible about politics. Her initial feeling was indignation at what she saw as their smug condescension. Then her common sense took over. If they *had* taken her seriously, her marriage would be in deep trouble. All in all, she decided that as long as she had Adrian, she would tolerate being condescended to.

Chapter 14

For leaving apart what honor it was to all of us
to serve such a lord as he whom I declared unto
you right now, every man conceived in his
mind an high contentation every time we came
into the duchess' sight.

—*The Book of the Courtier*

The unofficial government convention broke up at
the end of August with everyone looking forward
to pleasant leisure doings in the country. It appeared that it was the custom for hostesses to entertain large parties of people at their estates for a
week or more at a time. At first Tracy was somewhat dismayed to hear this, but Adrian assured her
that they would be spending a quiet month or two
at Steyning Castle before undertaking any more so-
cializing. She was delighted to hear this news; the
last month had been rather a strain.

Aside from the politics, there were other aspects
to life in English high society that Tracy found
strange and upsetting. The political issue appeared
to have been solved, but other problems remained.

For example, the amount of gambling that went on in her husband's world shocked her.

Tracy was a Yankee; she had a value for money. She knew where it came from—it came from hard work and effort. The sight of dozens of glittering aristocrats sitting up all night over a table of faro winning and losing fantastic sums of money disturbed her profoundly. Her husband did not seem to be interested in gambling, but she was uneasy. She said something of the sort to him once, tentatively and had been surprised by the abruptness of his response. She said nothing more to him about gambling but was uneasier still.

The other aspect of English upper class life that shocked her was the promiscuity. She did not think she would ever in her life forget the casual words of Lady Fanny Melburn when she answered Tracy's question about the identity of a very pretty young woman who was talking to the Duke. "Oh, that's Sophia Hawley. One of the Hawlian Miscellany, you know."

Tracy did not know. "The Hawlian Miscellany?" she asked, puzzled.

"The Hawley family," her informant answered readily. "The children of the Countess of Cambridge." Lady Fanny laughed lightly. "They are called the Hawlian Miscellany on account of the variety of fathers alleged to be responsible for their existence."

Tracy was horrified. She was a daughter of Puritan New England. Marital infidelity was almost beyond the scope of her comprehension. Yet, once her eyes were opened, she saw it all around her in London. Among married women the practice of having lovers was too common even to stir much comment. The only rule, it seemed, was that one must keep up appearances.

This was a subject she never broached to Adrian. She was afraid to. She was afraid to find out what he thought on the subject.

She was very glad to be going home to Steyning Castle. She wanted to have him to herself for awhile.

However, life at Steyning Castle was not quite the reprise of her honeymoon that Tracy had hoped for. For one thing, Steyning Castle was a very much larger establishment than Thorn Manor. Tracy had been stunned to drive up to the front door of her new home and find forty people waiting for her on the lawn. They were the servants the Duke explained to her kindly, and Tracy felt her jaw drop. At home she had had a housekeeper, a cook, a waitress and a chambermaid.

At Steyning Castle she had a housekeeper, a butler and a cook, as well as housemaids, footmen, coachmen, pantry boys, scullery maids and still-room maids. There were grooms for the stables and gardeners for the gardens. Tracy was overwhelmed by the sheer numbers. "I don't see how anyone can say there's an employment problem in England," she said to her husband. "Half of the country appears to work for you!"

She renewed her acquaintance with the Duke's sister, who was reserved but shyly friendly, and made the acquaintance of Mary's governess, Miss Alden. Miss Alden was a pleasant, intelligent woman of about thirty, and Tracy had great hopes of making a friend of her. However, to Tracy's dismay, the English consciousness of class interfered again. Even when they were conversing alone together about books, two women who had quite a lot in common, Miss Alden always made it clear that she knew that Tracy was the Duchess and she just a governess. Miss Alden never sat until Tracy was seated, never spoke until Tracy was finished speaking, never disagreed with any opinion Tracy might advance. Tracy felt as if she were caught in a cobweb of convention and protocol from which, much as she tried to struggle free, escape was impossible. She was the Duchess. The social distinction between her and the governess was too great to be overcome. She found the whole relationship very depressing.

Always at the back of her mind was the thought of her father. She did not consciously think of him all the time; indeed she tried not to. But the awareness of him and his illness was always there, a dull ache that became noticeable as soon as she was quiet and had time to remember. She wrote him long, newsy letters full of cheerfulness. And she cried when she folded them up to be sent.

There was another reason as well for the unsteadiness of her emotions. She thought she was with child. For the time being she kept her suspicions to herself. She did not want to tell the Duke until she was certain. Having a child would be a very important matter to him; she did not want to make a mistake.

She was certain of its importance although he had said nothing to her on the subject. He rarely spoke about the things that deeply mattered to him.

For all his charm and his instinct for relations, he was a very reserved man. For instance, he rarely ever mentioned his years in the army. Only once had she gotten an inkling of how he felt about the war. Lord Mulhaven had been talking about the military situation in Greece and had asked the Duke's opinion. "About war I agree with Wellington," her husband had answered shortly. "The only thing as bad as defeat is victory." And he had removed himself from the conversation.

Tracy respected his reticences. He had been an exceptionally good soldier she had discovered from sources other than himself, but the war had evidently left some scars. To her mind, a war *should* leave some scars, and his sensitivity only increased her admiration for him.

She admired him, she loved him, but he seemed more than ever obscure to her. He was as busy at Steyning Castle as he had been in London. He was a landlord on a scale unheard of in America, even in the South. He was Lord Warden of the Cinque Ports and as such presided over the local court of Shepway as chief magistrate. All this was in addition to his work for the government. The extent of his duties and responsibilities staggered her.

It was the precise nature of her own duties and responsibilities that remained unclear. Adrian always managed to find a part of the day to take her driving. He held a Public Day and introduced her to his tenants. He appeared to expect no more of her than that she be an ornament to his home, but that was not a position that overly appealed to Tracy.

She seemed to be so extraneous to his life and his activities. She wanted to share with him some of his problems at home since she was so unable to share in his political life. He was often closeted for hours at a time with his man of business and estate managers, but when she asked him what they spent so many hours doing he had answered with unusual shortness, "I am trying to rectify the neglect of generations. It is not an edifying job, I may say." His attitude had not encouraged further inquiry and Tracy, feeling rather snubbed, had said nothing more on the subject.

Clearly, he did not want her to intrude into his domain. He was also, equally clearly, a very busy man who did not have the day to devote to entertaining his wife. She had too much time on her hands and began, tentatively at first, to take up the reins of her household. Here she met with rather more success. Mrs. Map, the housekeeper, was very pleasant and the servants adored the new Duchess. She was so lovely, so friendly, so interested. She noticed them. She noticed Molly, the sixteen-year-old scullery maid who was red-eyed from crying because she was homesick; she noticed the gardener's assistant whose face was swollen with toothache; she noticed the lumpy mattresses in the servants' wing and ordered new ones.

She was shocked by what she regarded as the servility of the British working class and spoke her mind forcibly to Miss Alden one afternoon. Mary was out riding and Tracy and the governess were having tea in the library. "I'll tell you what I think of the whole English servant system, Miss Alden," she said, angrily stirring sugar into her tea. "I think it is disgusting." She had just sent the gardener's assistant to the dentist, and she was really disturbed.

Miss Alden looked startled. "I don't think I understand, Your Grace," she replied cautiously.

Tracy told her about the morning's incident. "*Why* didn't that child say anything about his tooth?" she asked rhetorically and then answered herself. "Because he didn't think he was important enough to matter, that's why." She put down her cup with some abruptness. "An American would look you right in the eye, tell you he had a toothache, and damn well expect you to pay attention. And if you didn't, he'd soon find another job."

"There aren't that many jobs available in England, Your Grace," said Miss Alden softly.

"So it seems. And the ones that are available all seem to involve creeping about under the feet of somebody else. It all makes me terribly uncomfortable."

Miss Alden looked at Tracy for a moment in silence. "I hadn't thought of it like that," she said slowly. "As an American I suppose it is rather difficult to adapt to our ways."

Tracy met the governess' eyes, her own very somber. Making one more attempt to break through the class barrier between them, she said, "I could use a friend, Miss Alden."

After a moment the older woman smiled. "I should be happy to be your friend, Your Grace."

"Thank God!" Tracy said devoutly. Miss Alden laughed and Tracy went on. "Please, won't you call me Tracy? There is hardly a soul in this whole country who calls me by my own name. It makes me feel very lonely sometimes."

"All right," said Miss Alden, hesitating. "Tracy."

Tracy smiled her irresistible smile. "It is not that I mean to complain, Elizabeth, but everything is still very strange to me. And I don't like to bother the Duke with all my little problems. He is so very busy, you see."

Miss Alden did see. For the first time she saw Tracy as she was; not the Duchess, but a young girl who found herself in a strange land far from all the people she had always known and understood. She was so beautiful and seemed so assured; Miss Alden had forgotten that after all she was only nineteen. "I shall always be happy to try to sort things out for you, Tracy," she said gently.

"Thank you so much, Elizabeth." Tracy's eyes moved beyond Miss Alden's shoulder and her smile warmed to radiance. The governess knew, without looking, who had come into the room behind her.

"Would you like to go for a drive with me, *ma mie?*" a soft, familiar voice inquired.

"I'd love to," said Tracy and as Miss Alden watched from the window a few minutes later, the Duke and Duchess drove together down the wide drive. Tracy was looking at her husband and laughing at something he had said to her. Watching them, Miss Alden felt a sharp pang of envy and her sympathy for Tracy considerably lessened. How could one feel sorry for a girl who was married to the Duke of Hastings?

Chapter 15

But speaking of the beauty that we mean,
which is only it that appeareth in bodies, and
especially in the face of man, and moveth this
fervent coveting which we call love . . .
— *The Book of the Courtier*

Toward the end of September Tracy told her husband the news she had been harboring for almost two months. They had had an especially pleasant day, driving into Brighton where Adrian had shown her the sights, particularly the Regent's Palace, which she had found unbelievable. They returned home for a late dinner together and then went to bed.

It had started to rain shortly after their return home, but the night was warm and the Duke had opened the window. Lying close along his body in the sweet, damp night air, Tracy felt more peaceful and happy than she had for many weeks. Her eyes closed, she listened to the slowing beat of his heart. "Adrian?" she murmured.

His hand was slowly caressing her hair. "Mmm?" he said deeply.

"I'm going to have a baby."

He didn't say anything, but the hand that was stroking her hair stilled. After a minute she raised her head and looked into the dark dark blue of his eyes. "Are you pleased?'" she asked softly.

"Very pleased." He spoke slowly, gravely. "Are you certain?"

"Yes. I went to see Dr. Brixton yesterday. It will be in March." Satisfied by what she saw on his face, she rested her head once more on his shoulder. "It will be a boy," she murmured contentedly.

"Why do you say that, *ma mie?*"

"Because you will want a boy. And you always get what you want."

At that he laughed, deep down in his throat. "I begin to think you may be right," he answered and, very gently, he kissed the top of her head. In a few minutes she was asleep.

She had pleased him with her news, and she wanted very much to please him. But still, there was so much about him she did not understand. He came to her in the library the next morning and said, "You must write to tell your father."

"Yes." She looked down at the book she was holding to have an excuse to keep her face hidden.

"Tell him if it is a boy we shall call him William."

"Oh, Adrian." She looked up at him, all efforts at privacy forgotten. He was standing by the window, dressed for riding in buckskins and worn but polished boots. The sun gilded his face and drew sparks of chestnut from his dark brown hair. "Thank you," she said softly.

He was looking right at her but, suddenly, and without his eyes even flickering, the shutters came down across his face. He seemed all at once a thousand miles away. "There is no cause for you to thank me," he said in measured tones. "The debt is all mine."

It frightened and hurt her when he closed up against her like this. She did not know what to say but sat looking at him out of troubled, golden eyes. He seemed to sense her distress because after a minute he smiled and held out his arms. She ran to him with wild relief, melted, as ever, by the power of his touch.

She decided she would learn to ride. Adrian spent a good part of his day in the saddle and she thought if she rode she could perhaps accompany him occasionally. She asked Mary to teach her.

It was to be a secret from Adrian. She wanted to surprise him with a *fait accompli* and Mary entered enthusiastically into her plan. The two girls would sneak out to the stables in the morning when the Duke was closeted with his men of business or out on the estate, Tracy dressed in one of Mary's habits, and Mary would give her a lesson. As Tracy was naturally athletic and fearless, she learned very quickly. Soon she had graduated from the longe line to circling the paddock on her own. By the end of the second week she was cantering with graceful confidence and Mary was saying she was almost ready for Adrian to see.

As it turned out, they didn't have a chance to

surprise him; he surprised them. Mary was standing in the middle of the paddock one cloudy morning watching Tracy walk her black gelding along the fence. "All right," Mary called, "pick up your canter." Tracy squeezed and lifted and the horse obediently went into motion. "No, no," Mary called, "wrong lead. Try again." Tracy pulled the horse up, again gave the signals, and this time Mary said, "That's it."

Tracy was busy shortening her reins when she heard a voice, quiet but perfectly audible, cut across the paddock. "What do you think you are doing?" It was Adrian.

Tracy pulled up in surprise and rocked a little in the saddle. He came across the paddock and took a firm grip on her bridle. "Get off," he said tersely.

He looked like a stranger; she had never seen that expression in his eyes before. She got off the horse.

When she was standing beside him he said again, "What do you think you are doing?" She realized, with an odd sense of shock, that he was angry.

"Mary is teaching me how to ride, Adrian," she replied steadily. "We were going to surprise you."

He turned his eyes to his sister, who was looking white faced and bewildered. "I don't suppose you knew," he said to her. "Tracy is expecting a baby."

Mary turned even whiter. "Oh my God. No, Adrian, I didn't know."

He nodded. "Take the horse back to the stable, Mary." His sister moved instantly to follow his command. "Come with me," he said to his wife. "I'll drive you back to the house."

Tracy fell into step with him, but she found, as

she kept up beside him, that she herself was becoming very angry. She waited until he helped her into the curricle and then said, her own voice icy and dangerous, "What is the matter with you? If I want to learn to ride a horse, then I will damn well learn. I don't need your permission!"

He didn't answer, but after a minute he turned his horses off the path to the Castle and onto the path that led through the park. They drove for five minutes in silence, Tracy rigidly upright beside Adrian, until he finally pulled up in the shelter of some large trees that edged the ornamental lake. He stared at the water, his profile unreadable. "I'm sorry, *ma mie*," he said at last, sounding very weary. "I did not mean to be so abrupt."

She was immediately disarmed, as only he could leave her. She shivered a little. "But what is the matter, Adrian? I thought you would be so pleased. You love to ride yourself."

He still did not look at her. "My mother had a fall from a horse when she was carrying a child." He spoke very quietly, his eyes on the gray water. "She miscarried and it killed her."

"Oh," said Tracy, her eyes wide with horror and sympathy. "I'm so sorry. I did not know."

He turned and took her in his arms. "I don't want you to ride, *ma mie*," he murmured into her hair. "Not now."

She rested her head against his shoulder with a movement that indicated to them both that she would not resist. "I won't," she said. "I'm sorry."

They stayed so for several long minutes. Then he said, "After the baby is born, if you still want to learn, *I* will teach you."

Reluctantly she raised her head. "I'll hold you to that," she promised.

Expertly he backed the horses, turned them and started once again toward the house. The sun suddenly came out and she glanced up in surprise. There was a patch of clear sky right above them. They drove in silence for a minute and then he said, "Shall I tell you something?"

She turned to look at him and found him watching her. His eyes were a much darker blue than the sky. "What?" she asked curiously.

He looked back at the road. His profile was regally calm, but to the knowledgeable eye amusement lurked in the curve of his mouth. "I get seasick," he said softly.

"No!" Tracy's infectious laugh rippled out. "Do you really, Adrian?"

"I do."

"That's marvelous." Tracy continued to laugh. "That restores my faith in human fallibility."

"I thought it might," he agreed serenely and Tracy laughed again.

"Seasick!"

He looked at her, a smile glimmering in those remarkable eyes of his, and she smiled back, restored by his infinite tact and generosity to her old equilibrium and self-esteem.

Chapter 16

He was indeed the Duke.
—Shakespeare

The letters Tracy received from her father told her nothing about his health. That they came regularly, on almost every ship from America, led her to believe that he must still be fairly strong. So when Adrian asked if she wished to go to the Bridgewaters' chief estate, Matching Castle, for a house party in late October, she assented.

She was feeling very well, having none of the uncomfortable side effects of pregnancy. And, aside from his interdiction about riding, the Duke made no attempts to hamper any of her activities. She was grateful for his lack of fussiness, particularly since she knew how important the coming child was to him. It would have driven her wild to be treated as an invalid.

Matching Castle was very grand and Lady Bridgewater had collected a party every bit as grand as its surroundings. There was the Prime Minister, four Cabinet ministers, four government ministers and half a dozen other members of Parliament as well as a few assorted lords who were high placed enough not to be required to do anything to account for their existences. These gentlemen had all brought their wives and daughters, a collection of some of the most brilliant and beautiful ladies to be found in English society.

Their first day at Matching Castle had passed rather auspiciously for both the Duke and the Duchess. Lord Bridgewater had been manifestly delighted to see Tracy. The Duke's uncle-by-marriage was a fussy, clever, popular, conscientious man, who had been born into the semi-purple of ministerial influence. He had formed a part of the government ever since Lord Liverpool had taken office, and he would undoubtedly continue to be one of its mainstays until that far distant occasion when the Tories went out of power.

When Tracy came into the drawing room with Adrian before dinner, Lord Bridgewater had instantly moved to greet her. In a few minutes she was part of a group of elderly nobles, all of whom were beaming at her in great pleasure. Lord Bridgewater took her into dinner, where she sat at his right and next to Lord Liverpool. Both of those gentlemen appeared to hang on her every word.

The truth was that Tracy was extremely popular with the male segments of society, a fact her husband had long recognized. He watched her now, when he had a minute to spare from his own dinner partners, and there was a smile in his eyes. Her political opinions didn't matter a particle. What people responded to were her vitality, her positiveness, her high-hearted approach to life. She was like a fresh sea breeze blowing into a stuffy, enclosed place, he thought now, watching her treat Lord Liverpool to what one of the Duke's more highly placed diplomatic colleagues had once called the prettiest smile in Europe. Adrian's own smile spread from his eyes to his lips. Everything seemed clearer and brighter and freer when Tracy was present, he thought. No one cared at all that she was in favor of abolishing the House of Lords.

Lady Bridgewater was more critical of the new young Duchess than either her husband or her nephew. She had been responsible for marrying Adrian and she felt herself responsible for the success of that marriage. And when she talked of successful marriages, Lady Bridgewater did not talk in terms of affection. A successful marriage to her mind was one which adhered to convention and furthered family prosperity and prestige. Tracy had certainly contributed to family prosperity; Lady Bridgewater wished to ensure that she also exhibited the other necessary virtues.

It did not disturb her that Tracy attracted men so easily. Lady Bridgewater was a typical woman of the world, more eighteenth than nineteenth century in her thinking. It was not wrong for a woman to have lovers. What she thought inexcusable was for a woman to neglect her duty to her family or to act in such a way as to outrage social standards. She determined, now that she had a week of unlimited access to the young Duchess, to impart some of her code into Tracy's pretty but ignorant ear.

For Tracy, the house party became more upsetting with every passing day. On the one hand she had Lady Bridgewater, with her air of indescribable distinction, imparting to her a philosophy of life and marriage that Tracy found appalling in its immorality, and on the other hand she had the increasing fear that it was a philosophy in which her husband might share.

The crux of her unhappiness was a guest at the house party, the Comtesse d'Aubigny, the wife of a French diplomat. The Comtesse was very French, very clever, very brilliant, very charming and very beautiful. She was, in short, a *femme du monde*, a highly developed specimen of a highly developed type, a type that was tremendously alien to Tracy.

When the Comtesse had first seen Adrian she had put out her hand to him without moving from her place, and he had gone to kiss her fingers immediately. That they knew each other well, was clear to Tracy. The Comtesse called him *Monseigneur* and talked to him in a sophisticated ripple of small talk that made him laugh. Tracy distrusted her instantly, a distrust that only grew as the week progressed.

She had come up to Tracy after dinner on the first evening of her arrival, all charm and smiles. "So, you are the American girl who has married *Monseigneur de Hythe*—ah, no, he is *Monseigneur de Hastings* now, no?"

"Yes," replied Tracy briefly. "He is and I am."

The Comtesse sighed with melancholy charm. "How we miss him in Paris. It is all so flat now that he is gone."

"I rather doubt if Paris could ever be flat, Comtesse," said Tracy dryly.

The Comtesse made a graceful gesture. "But it is. Decidedly. All the woman, they weep nightly." She shook her head. "You are a fortunate girl, *Duchesse*." She tilted her head to one side. "And you are very pretty. Yes, one can see why he married you."

Tracy could feel her temper rising. Who *was* this woman and what had she been to Adrian? "I had no idea that Adrian had left half of France in sackcloth and ashes when he left," she said tartly and the Comtesse laughed.

"He did, *madame*. I assure you, he did."

The gentlemen came into the room at that moment and Tracy stood up. "I am so sorry for you all," she said sweetly, "but it must have been heaven for Adrian," and she walked over to the door to join her husband as he entered.

She felt such a foreigner. She was surrounded by other measures, a different scale of values from the one with which she had lived all her life. The rapacious worldliness of all these great people rasped on her spirit. It was not a worldliness that her husband appeared to share, but as the week went by she began to doubt him. She watched him. She watched the Comtesse d'Aubigny, her clothes stylishly worn, her cleverness gracefully displayed, her social utility brilliantly exemplified. It began to seem to her that it was such a one as the Comtesse that Adrian ought to have married.

It was not that he neglected her. At night, lying in his arms, carried away by him to the farthest reaches of passion and surrender, she could not doubt him. But by day, she did. He was so practiced a man of the world, so supple in his response to the various nuances of social atmosphere, so able to adapt himself. Did he just show to her the things she would want to see?

It was a doubt that Tracy could not live with. The one thing that would kill her was dishonesty. She resolved to drag her suspicions out into the open, to tell him of her fears.

It was a confrontation that she put off for the duration of the visit. It was not until they were in their coach, away from the corroding atmosphere of Matching Castle, that she dared to bring up the subject that had destroyed the pleasure of her visit. "The Comtesse d'Aubigny told me that all the women in Paris weep nightly since you left," she began in a small voice.

He laughed easily. "She exaggerates, *ma mie*," he said. "I'm quite sure no one wept to see me leave."

Tracy kept her eyes on her lap. "You seemed to know her very well."

"Yes, we were quite good friends in Paris."

Tracy took a deep breath. "Did you make love to her, Adrian?"

"Ah," the Duke said quietly. "Now that is a question a gentleman never answers."

"And it is a question, I gather, that a lady never asks." She turned and looked for a minute directly at him, then she dropped her eyes again. "But a lady—a married lady—can make love with a man who is not her husband. *That* does not stop her from being a lady."

He exhaled a long breath that was like a guarded sigh. "Paris is not New England, Tracy."

"No. Nor is London. I have ears. And eyes. I have seen what goes on."

He put his arm around her and drew her close. For the first time she did not immediately relax in his embrace. She sat stiffly, afraid that he was not going to answer her, that he had resorted to familiar magic to avoid responding to her questions. After a minute he said very seriously, "What I did before I met and married you does not concern you, Tracy." She sat silent, resisting the possessive curve of his arm, the pressure of his body against hers. "But I am a married man now, and things are different from what they were when I was in Paris. If you don't trust me to realize that, then we do not have what I thought we did."

"I thought we had a marriage. But in New England we take marriage more seriously than you appear to take it here." Still she resisted her husband's grasp. "For me, you see, marriage means fidelity," she said.

She was looking straight ahead of her in the dimness of the carriage. He reached over with his free hand and took her fingers in a firm grasp. She looked down at his narrow hand; she loved the long fingers, the shape and color of the immaculate nails. She bit her lower lip to keep it from quivering. "Then let us have a New England marriage," he said.

A little of the rigidity left her back. "I'm willing if you are," she said in a muffled voice.

"I won't find it at all difficult," he answered promptly. "I find I've lost all my interest in women who are not my wife." She turned her face into his shoulder. "And," he continued, "if I ever find you acting the role of a *femme du monde*, I shall beat you."

"I'll lend you the whip," said Tracy into his shoulder. He began to laugh and after a minute, shakily, she joined in.

Chapter 17

Afterward let him obey, please, and honor with
all reverence his woman, and reckon her more
dear to him than his own life, and prefer all
her commodities and pleasures before his own,
and love no less in her the beauty of the mind
than of the body.
                                   —*The Book of the Courtier*

If someone had told the Duke six months previously that he would be promising absolute fidelity
to his wife and meaning every word of it, he
would have been amazed. When he had decided to
make Tracy his wife he had had every intention of
being a good husband, but his idea of the duties of
a good husband did not—then—include the obliga-
tion of sexual fidelity. He had thought he and
Tracy had the basis of a successful marriage: he
brought to their union an ancient title and lineage
and she brought beauty and money. Each had
something to offer that the other lacked. Many successful marriages had begun with less.

But his marriage, and his wife, had not been

what he expected. For one thing, she had not married him to become the Duchess of Hastings. She had married him for himself; there was no other reason he could find for her action. She loved him. He did not doubt that, and the thought was ineffably sweet to him.

He had married her for her money. As the weeks went by and he fell ever more deeply under her spell, that thought began to bother him. It had not bothered him at the time of his marriage; he had thought then that he was making a bargain. But the bargain had been made with Mr. Bodmin, not with his daughter.

She had asked him once, point blank, with her usual devastating honesty, if he was interested in her money. He had reassured her and the question had not come up again. He did not ever want it to come up again. It was a subject upon which he was extremely sensitive.

Mr. Bodmin's settlement had been hugely generous. It had needed to be; the condition of the Duke's estates was worse than he had realized. His morning sessions with his man of business and his estate agents left him feeling very bleak indeed. And very angry. His ancestors, in his opinion, deserved to have been horsewhipped.

He did not want his wife to know the extent of his embarrassments. Thanks to Bodmin money, they would all be rectified. But he did not want her to know how necessary that money had been.

Quite simply, he loved her. He loved her intensely, with all the passion and the possessiveness that was in his nature. When he told her he had lost interest in all women who were not his wife he had spoken the simple truth. Next to Tracy's glowing vitality all other women paled into insignificance. He loved her and he wanted no shadow cast on his marriage.

Tracy, fortunately, seemed sublimely unconscious of money. She was the daughter of a rich man, but she herself had never handled much money; the simple life in Salem had not lent itself to lavish expenditure. She had an allowance from the money her father settled on her at her marriage and from that allowance she bought clothes and books. She was thrifty in a way the Duke was not accustomed to see in the women he had known. She might spend a great deal of money on a dress, but the dress was worn with more frequency than another woman with her money would have worn it. It was also, to the Duke's mind, invariably more attractive than the dresses worn by those other women.

The subject of money never came up between them. He paid all the household expenses, an arrangement Tracy never questioned. When she bought something for the house he told her to have the bills sent to him, and she did so unhesitatingly. In fact, their arrangement was very familiar to her; at home her father had handled all the financial matters of the household.

She was the wife he wanted. It did not bother him at all that she didn't agree with his politics. He didn't want a political wife like his aunt was. Tracy's interest was in people, not politics, and in the matter of character her judgment was usually excellent.

He had first realized this a few weeks after their

marriage when they had returned from a diplomatic reception at the Russian Embassy. Prince Vassily, one of the new attachés, had devoted himself to the young Duchess for a good part of the evening. The Prince was handsome, charming, vivacious and ambitious. The Duke asked his wife what she thought of him on their way home in the carriage.

"Prince Vassily has a delightfully open, honest manner," she said, "but I wouldn't trust him farther than I could see him."

He was surprised by the shrewdness of her observation and by its accuracy. He had known the Prince in Paris and had come to the same conclusion. But it had taken him weeks to see the young man's deviousness; it had taken his wife less than an hour.

She was accurate about a number of other people whom the Duke knew, and he had come to the comfortable conclusion that if he were ever in doubt on a matter of a person's trustworthiness, he could rely on his wife's judgment. She laughed with them and charmed them; she talked about books and music and theatre and voyages to the South Seas; and she got their measure.

He knew her father was on her mind and he did everything he could think of to keep her occupied. He took her driving as often as he could and he encouraged her friendship with Miss Alden. When they returned from Matching Castle he had the happy notion of complaining about the state of the linen in his own home and that triggered Tracy's houswifely instincts. She began a campaign to brighten up and refurbish the house, and he agreed with all her suggestions. It was going to cost him rather a lot of money, he thought philosophically, but his wife's peace of mind was worth it.

On November 28 a letter arrived from America. It was from Tracy's maternal uncle, Francis Breen. Her father was dead.

Her initial response was a strange feeling of peace; the waiting, the wondering, the restlessness, were over. Adrian bundled her up in a warm cloak, wrapped a blanket around her legs, and took her for a long drive. They went down to the sea. She sat next to him in the curricle and gazed out at the sparkling water off Beachy Head. Her eyes misted over and she quoted softly from Robert Thorne's letter to Henry VIII: " 'There is no land unhabitable, or Sea innavigable.' That was one of Papa's favorite sayings. He loved the ocean so." She closed her eyes and put her cheek against his shoulder.

He did not answer but put his arm around her and drew her close. The long firm pressure of his arm, the feel of his warm body against hers, comforted her more than any words. "Adrian," she murmured and for a moment he held her closer. Then he turned the horses and started the long drive back to Steyning Castle.

Shortly thereafter Mr. Bodmin's London lawyers contacted Tracy. "Papa had his will drawn up in America and sent to Mr. Spencer in London," she said to the Duke in a carefully collected voice. "Mr. Spencer says that he wishes to make me acquainted with the contents. He will come down to Sussex at our convenience."

The Duke had just come in from a ride and now

he laid his gloves down on a table. "Write to tell him to come next Tuesday," he said calmly. "It will be as well to get the business over with before Christmas."

"Yes," said Tracy. She felt suddenly old and sad and tired. "A will. I had forgotten there would have to be a will. It makes it so final somehow. It makes him seem so—dead."

Mr. Spencer came, a surprisingly young and vigorous man. Tracy had vaguely supposed that all lawyers were old and dusty and dried up. Mr. Spencer's firm, it turned out, had handled many of William Bodmin's affairs in the past. He had been personally acquainted with Tracy's father and sincerely expressed to her his sense of sorrow at her loss.

They went into the library and Mr. Spencer read the will out loud to Tracy and the Duke. Tracy made an effort to listen, but her attention kept wandering. The legal terms, the sums of money, it all seemed to have so little to do with her father. Adrian will handle it, she thought, as the lawyer went on about millions and funds and trusts. She looked alertly at Mr. Spencer's big, fair face and thought instead of Salem and the churchyard where her father had been buried.

When Mr. Spencer had finished he asked if she had any questions. "No, no, none, thank you," she assured him. "I'm sure His Grace will know what to do about it all."

Mr. Spencer gave her a puzzled look. "I think, my love, you and I ought to discuss what Mr. Spencer has told us for a little, and then, if you

have any questions, you can ask them after dinner."
The Duke nodded courteously at the lawyer. "If
that would be convenient?"

"Of course, Your Grace," the man said quickly,
beginning to gather his papers.

Tracy smiled at him warmly. "We dine at seven,
Mr. Spencer. I'll have Wilton take you upstairs
now."

"Thank you, Your Grace," Mr. Spencer said, visibly moved by that amazing smile.

The Duke watched him leave the room under
the stately escort of Wilton, then he turned to his
wife. "Did you listen to anything that man said?"

"Well . . ." She bit her lip. "No."

"You should have. He was talking about a great
deal of money, Tracy. Over ten million dollars, I
gathered."

Tracy looked at him in genuine bewilderment.
"But, Adrian, *I* don't know what to do with money
like that. All I've ever had is an allowance. Aren't
you going to handle it?"

"I can't."

"But why?"

"If you had listened, *ma mie*, you would have
discovered that the money is safely secured to you
and to your children after you. Your father seems
to have invested it wisely, and you will receive a
regular "allowance" from the principal—an allowance a good deal larger than what you are accustomed to, I daresay." He leaned a little forward,
looking directly into the clear hazel of her eyes.
"The money is yours," he said steadily. "It is very
carefully safeguarded for you. I cannot touch it."

Tracy looked back at him, a small frown between her brows. "Why did Papa do that?" she asked at last.

He sat back, faint amusement in his eyes. "So that if I ever took to getting drunk and beating you, you could walk away with all your millions safely in your pocket, I expect."

She looked at him reflectively. Then, raising an eyebrow, "You knew he was going to do this, didn't you?"

"It is not an uncommon action for him to have taken."

"Was it your idea?"

He compressed his lips. "Let us say, both your father and I agreed that this would be the best way."

She nodded thoughtfully, her mind not on the ten million dollars she had just inherited, but on her husband's motivation in urging the arrangements he had. "It won't be so difficult," he said encouragingly. "The lawyers will handle nearly everything. All you'll have to do is sign your name." He paused, frowned, then added, "But don't sign anything until after I've seen it. I'm sure Spencer is first rate, but one can't be too careful."

"Yes, Adrian," she said absently, still regarding him wonderingly.

His undisturbed manner gave nothing away. "Shall we go and change for dinner?" he asked, and held out his hand to assist her.

Chapter 18

But such was the respect we bore to the duchess'
will that the selfsame liberty was a very great
bridle. Neither was there any that thought it
not the greatest pleasure he could have in the
world to please her and the greatest grief to
offend her.

—*The Book of the Courtier*

Christmas was a quiet, family time at Steyning
Castle. Even Lady Bridgewater did not expect the
Duchess, who was six months pregnant and had
just lost her father, to undertake any social obliga-
tions. In consequence, Tracy had a happier Christmas than she had thought possible. Her pregnancy
helped to cushion her from some of the grief she
would otherwise have suffered for her father, the
coming baby being very much in her mind and
heart most of the time.

She was reflecting on her own surprisingly tran-
quil state of mind one morning a few days after
Christmas when the mail brought her an unexpected reminder of the past. She and the Duke

were having breakfast together in her sitting room, a comfortable habit they had kept up after their honeymoon. Adrian was reading the newspaper and she was idly sorting through her letters when she came upon one that riveted her attention. It was from America. She opened it slowly. The handwriting was familiar and one glance at the signature confirmed her suspicion. It was from Adam Lancaster. She put down her coffee cup and read it through.

It was a letter of sympathy and pertained mainly to her father. Adam, she knew, had always thought very highly of William Bodmin, and his words moved Tracy very much. It was the concluding paragraph that made her uncomfortable.

"Your marriage was a source of great happiness to your father," he wrote. "I hope it is the same to you. My own feelings for you have not changed, Trace. I love you and I desire most of all that you should be happy." She bit her lip, feeling guilty once again about Adam. He signed himself "ever your devoted friend."

Her husband had put aside his paper and was watching her. "Is anything amiss, *ma mie?*" he asked quietly and Tracy jumped noticeably.

"No." She flushed a little. For some reason she did not want to tell Adrian about Adam. "It's from a friend of mine in Salem," she said quickly. "He wrote to offer his sympathy about my father."

"I see," he answered. He had been quick to pick up that "he," but with the beautiful manners that were such an innate part of him, he forbore to question her further. She put the letter down and began to chat to him with cheerful determination.

A week later the doctor came to check on her progress. She was having an extremely easy pregnancy and only recently had begun to assume a noticeable bulk. Dr. Brixton was pleased with her health and stayed to talk sympathetically about her father's death. The Duke was waiting for the doctor downstairs and invited him into the library for a glass of wine. Adrian was very careful not to annoy Tracy by being over solicitous, but he was also very careful to assure himself that such solicitude was not necessary.

"Her Grace is doing splendidly," Dr. Brixton said with a smile. "She is perfectly healthy. A great deal healthier, I may say, than many women who are not enceinte."

The Duke gave Dr. Brixton a glass of Madeira. "I am happy to hear that." He sipped his own wine. "Do you have any recommendations, Doctor?"

"No, Your Grace, I don't think so. Her father's death was a misfortune, of course, but she seems to be accepting it well."

"Yes. I believe Her Grace has a great deal of resiliency," said the Duke.

The doctor nodded. "We talked for a little about her father and I gather she might have inherited that trait from him. He appears to have been a remarkable man."

"I believe he was," his son-in-law said sincerely.

"Her Grace told me that she was so glad he lived to know about the child. 'Papa was a secret snob,' she said. 'He was thrilled by the thought of his grandson being a future duke.' I believe she feels comforted that she had given him that, at least, before he died."

There was the faintest of frowns on the Duke's handsome face. Dr. Brixton, noticing it, was afraid he had offended. He put down his wineglass. "Well, thank you for the refreshment, Your Grace," he said somewhat gruffly.

The Duke nodded a little absently but when Dr. Brixton moved to leave insisted upon escorting him to the front door. This courtesy considerably soothed the doctor's uneasiness and he left Steyning Castle in a gratified and comfortable state of mind.

The Duke's state of mind was not so easy. By itself, Dr. Brixton's comment about Tracy's happiness in pleasing her father would have meant nothing to him. But Adrian had not been able to get the letter from her American "friend" out of his mind; he had not been able to get the look on her face as she had read it out of his mind either. He had seen the letter once again on her dressing table when he had come looking for her and found the room empty. She had obviously been rereading it. He had stared at the bold, masculine handwriting on the envelope and the temptation to pick up the letter and read it had startled him with its intensity. It had taken great resolution to turn back to his own room and close the door.

All his life the Duke had had his own way with very little trouble. In fact, it is probably accurate to say that no one, with the exception of his father, had ever denied or thwarted him. Even his marriage had been easy.

Now, for the first time, he found himself wondering *why* it had been so easy. Tracy had not married him for his title. He had thought he knew why she married him, but he was beginning to doubt his own happy conclusion. The letter from America bothered him. A girl like Tracy—of course she had had suitors in her own country. How serious might they have been? And, most worrisome, for the first time he remembered that Tracy's father had been dying and that Tracy had known it. Mr. Bodmin had wanted this marriage. Mr. Bodmin had arranged it. Had Tracy simply married him to please her father?

He had never doubted her love, but now he began to wonder. She gave him what he had never gotten from any other woman, but then she was passionate by nature, he thought. And she was honest. If she made a bargain, she would give her best. But he did not want his marriage to be a bargain. He tried to put these uncomfortable doubts from his mind, but he was not wholly successful. It was too important a question for him to dismiss it so easily.

Tracy was completely unaware of the doubts her mysterious letter from America had raised in her husband's mind. She herself was feeling more secure in her marriage since their visit to Matching Castle. The terrible, menacing fear of his possible duplicity had been removed. No longer was she tormented by thoughts of another woman in his arms.

She thought, now, that he would be loyal to her. She was his wife. She was carrying his child. Adrian had a very strong sense of family. She would profit from that.

She enjoyed talking to Mary about her husband, and in so doing she discovered more about his character. Ever since the horseback riding lessons she and Mary had been friends and the long winter days saw them firmly cement that friendship. Adrian's sister was shy and reserved, but her feelings ran very deep and she was extremely attached to the Duke.

It was Mary who told her the details of her mother's death. "I was five at the time," she said, "but I remember the groom carrying her into the house. I remember the doctor running up the stairs. I was so frightened and lost. Then she died."

They were seated together in Tracy's sitting room with a warm fire blazing. Mary put down her needlework and stared at the flames. "I ran away and hid in the woods. Adrian came to find me. I can still remember how he sat next to me on a big rock and how he put his arm around me. I remember how comforting and warm his shoulder was. He said, 'Don't be afraid, Mary. I'll take care of you. You'll always have me.' " A faint smile lifted Mary's lips. "He seemed very old and very wise to me then, but he was only sixteen. And he kept his promise. He has always taken care of both Harry and me. When he was away in the Peninsula, and then in France, he wrote to me regularly every week."

"Did he indeed?" said Tracy thoughtfully. She took a few stitches and then looked up. "Why did he join the army, Mary? He was a very good soldier, I know, but it doesn't really seem like Adrian's kind of life."

"I think he went to get away from Papa," Mary

confessed. "They fought all the time. That is, Papa would shout and curse and Adrian would answer in that pleasant, controlled voice of his that always sends shivers up my spine."

Tracy frowned. "But what did they fight about?"

"Papa's gambling," said Mary grimly. "He gambled all the time. And he lost huge sums of money." She sighed. "It seems a terrible thing to say about one's father, Tracy, but I didn't like him very much." Then Mary reached out and put a comforting hand on Tracy's arm. "Adrian is not at all like Papa," she said reassuringly. "*He* will be a wonderful father, I'm sure. Just as he has been a wonderful brother."

"I'm sure he will be," said Tracy quietly and after a minute returned to her sewing.

Mary's revelations only confirmed what Tracy had long known. Adrian had married her for her father's money. She had seen the run-down state of the land and the cottages. She had seen the workmen descending in droves these last few months. She had heard the vicar after church thanking Adrian on behalf of the tenants for the repairs he was undertaking. She had realized that it must be Bodmin money that Adrian was using.

He had married her because he needed that money, but she thought he had come to care for her as well. Why should he not, she thought to herself in painful amusement, when but a single touch of his hand, of his lips, produced in her such absolute submission. She would do what he wanted to do, when he wanted to do it. He could not ask for a more pliable wife, nor one who adored him more abjectly. And she would give him a son. A son would bind him to her more firmly than anything else in the world.

So when he told her he would be faithful to her, she believed him. But she did not think that he loved her with a fraction of the helpless, powerful passion that she felt for him.

Chapter 19

"The engend'ring," quoth he, "of beauty in beauty aright were the engend'ring of a beautiful child in a beautiful woman; and I would think it a more manifest token a great deal that she loved her lover if she pleased him with this then with the sweetness of language you spoke of."

— *The Book of the Courtier*

The month of January went very slowly for Tracy. Parliament reopened and Adrian went up to London for days at a time. She missed him. She felt ugly and fat and horribly dull. She felt as if March would never ever come.

However, her boredom was soon alleviated, but not in a wholly pleasant manner. It was a cold, wet day in late January and she was breakfasting alone, the Duke being up in London. She picked up one of the newspapers, saw the headline, and went white and then red as she read the article.

General Andrew Jackson, on an expedition to West Florida, had arrested two British subjects as

157

spies. He had had the two men, a Scot named Arbuthnot and an ex-marine named Ambrister, tried
by an American military court and then shot. All of
this had occurred several months ago, but the news
had just hit England. And it had exploded like a
bombshell. The newspapers were all clamoring
for the government to take action against the
United States.

Tracy was terribly agitated. The Duke was in
London. Richard Rush, her Ambassador, was in
London. She decided that she had to go up to London too and rang the bell with great vigor to order
the carriage.

Wilton was almost as agitated as Tracy by her
order. He was quite sure the Duke would not want
his wife to be traveling and as he, a mere butler,
could certainly not prevent her, he went to the one
person whom he thought might have some success.
He went to Miss Alden. The governess thanked
him for his information and made her way with
some misgivings to the Duchess' bedroom.

She found Tracy pacing about like a caged tiger,
albeit a very pregnant caged tiger, as Emma dis-
tressfully packed her portmanteau. "Tracy, I must
speak to you," the governess said quietly. Tracy
merely shook her head and kept on pacing. Miss
Alden made a gesture to Emma, who turned and
hurried out of the room.

Tracy turned on the governess. "How dare you
send my maid away? I am going to London, Elizabeth. Haven't you read the papers? England is going to declare war on my country!"

"Yes, I have read the papers, but I feel quite certain that there will be no war. You know the English papers, Tracy! They always exaggerate."

Tracy's eyes were green as grass. "I don't know what to think and I am going to go where I can find out the truth of it. I want to talk to Mr. Rush. I want to see my husband." The room was electric with her alarm and her determination. Miss Alden was a little overwhelmed, but she made another effort.

"Tracy." Her voice was urgent. "Think. The Duke would not want you to travel, not in your conditon." That was the crux of the matter in fact. Miss Alden herself did not think a drive up to London would harm Tracy. But the Duke would be very angry if she went. Miss Alden was quite sure that some of that anger would be directed at herself for not stopping his wife from making what he would regard as a foolish and dangerous journey. She could not bear it if he were displeased or disappointed with her. Miss Alden had been aware for many months of the power of a pair of dark blue eyes, of the fascination of a face that resembled to her mind an engraving on a fine old coin. She wanted, very much, for him to think well of her. "His Grace will not like it," she repeated desperately.

"Then it's too bad about him," retorted his wife tersely and the door opened behind Miss Alden.

"Really, *ma mie*," an easy voice said in soft complaint, "that is hardly respectful of you."

"Adrian!" cried Tracy with intense relief. "I was going to come up to London to find you."

"Yes, well, that is hardly necessary now that I am here," he replied reasonably.

"Is there going to be a war?" She was rigid, her eyes still glitteringly green.

He looked profoundly surprised. "War? Of course there is not going to be a war. Good heavens, *ma mie*, you don't believe the papers, do you?" He walked across the room to take his wife in his arms as Miss Alden backed out the door. She went downstairs to cancel Tracy's order for the carriage only to find that the Duke had already done so. He had left London at the unheard-of hour of six in the morning in order to reach Steyning Castle by ten. He must have known how his wife would react to the newspapers. Miss Alden sighed with relief that the responsibility for Tracy was now off her shoulders.

It had taken all the Duke's skill to soothe and reassure his wife. It had taken a great deal of patience and forbearance as well. According to Tracy, Arbuthnot and Ambrister were scoundrels who had been stirring up the Indians along the American border. They deserved, in her vigorously voiced opinion, everything they had gotten. The Duke thought otherwise and in a frank conversation with Richard Rush he had gathered that the American government was not happy with Jackson's action but felt it had no choice but to stand behind its General.

It was not an opinion he could advance to Tracy. She was always slightly defensive about her country, always quick to detect smugness and condescension in the English attitude toward America, and on this issue she would admit no wrong. General Jackson was a hero and Arbuthnot and Ambrister were scoundrels and skunks. Period.

Her unreasonableness grated on the Duke's nerves, on his finer sensibility, but he displayed only infinite tact. He got Richard Rush to come down to Steyning Castle. He put in heroically long hours with the Cabinet in order to insure that the situation would *not* come to war, a possibility that was not as remote as he had implied to Tracy. In fact, months later Lord Castlereagh would say to Richard Rush that such was the temper of Parliament and such the feeling of the country that he believed war might have been produced by holding up a finger. That the finger was not held up, according to Castlereagh, was largely due to the Duke of Hastings.

It was a trying time for Adrian. On one hand he had his own countrymen, whose tempers were running very high over the "murders" of Arbuthnot and Ambrister. And on the other hand he had his wife, who kept telling him the English should see what it was like to try and live along a border where alien malcontents were stirring up Indian atrocities. It was all very wearing and made him realize for perhaps the first time that having an American wife was not all roses.

The crisis passed, however, and March arrived. International politics faded from Tracy's concern and approaching childbirth took their place. She made Dr. Brixton sit down and describe to her the whole process. He had been reluctant at first, afraid to frighten her, but she was adamant. "I can face anything if I know what it is," she said. "The unknown is far more frightening, I promise you." So he described the process of birth in detail and she listened attentively. She thought she was prepared.

Her imaginings, however, did not come close to the actual pain of the reality. The pain was terrible, so terrible that it swallowed her up, consumed her, so that she was not Tracy any more, but just pain. She moaned with it, writhed with it, all the time bearing down, trying to push the child out so that it would be over and the pain would stop.

Her labor began at five in the morning and the doctor arrived at six. As soon as Dr. Brixton arrived, with a woman to assist him, the Duke was banished. Mary had been sent to stay with Lady Bridgewater two weeks earlier because it was not considered suitable for a young girl to be in the house while a birth was in progress. Miss Alden had accompanied Mary and Harry was at school, so he was alone.

For the Duke it was an interminably long day. He breakfasted and then wrote letters in the library all morning. He walked around the garden for a while in the early afternoon and returned to the house and the library where he sat at his desk with estate work in front of him. He had been staring at the same paper for over an hour when there came a knock on the door and Dr. Brixton appeared. It was the second time the doctor had come to make a report.

"Yes?" the Duke asked sharply.

"It will be a while yet, Your Grace. It's a breech birth, I'm afraid."

"Breech birth? What is that?"

"The baby is coming out buttocks first instead of head first, Your Grace."

"Is that dangerous?"

"Not necessarily," the doctor said soothingly. "But it takes longer. The Duchess is being extremely cooperative. There is no cause for you to worry."

Tea was brought into the library at four and the Duke, his face expressionless, poured himself a cup, which he drank slowly, standing by the window. At five o'clock the door opened to reveal Dr. Brixton. "I am happy to tell you that you have a son," he said with a smile.

The Duke was standing in front of the fire. "And my wife?"

"The Duchess is very tired, Your Grace. It was not an easy birth, I can tell you that now. But there is no reason for her not to make a full recovery."

For the first time all day there was a flicker of expression in the Duke's eyes. He crossed the room to the doctor. "May I see her?"

Dr. Brixton nodded. "For a few minutes. She needs to sleep, Your Grace."

The Duke nodded. "I understand." He hesitated, as a thought struck him. "And what do *you* need, my dear man? A glass of wine? A brandy?"

The doctor laughed. "A glass of wine wouldn't come amiss, Your Grace. It was a long afternoon."

"Yes," said the Duke quietly as he pulled the bell. "It was." When a footman appeared he ordered a bottle of wine for the doctor and two glasses. "I'll join you shortly," he said with a faint smile and Dr. Brixton looked enormously pleased.

He walked with measured tread up the stairs and

along the corridor to Tracy's room. He stood for a minute in the doorway, watching her. She looked so slight in the big bed. "Adrian." Her voice was low and thin. He crossed the floor to her side and picked up her hand. She looked gray. Her beautiful tawny hair was dark with sweat.

He was holding her hand so tightly that Tracy felt the bones ache. "It was a long day, *ma mie*," he said.

She smiled a little. "Go look at your son."

He walked over to the cradle and stood for several minutes looking down. He thought of the months Tracy had toiled around, uncomfortable and unaccustomedly awkward. He thought of the long, long labor and the tiredness of her face. And out of it all—miraculously—had come this perfect baby. A son. Another Deincourt to carry on his name and his heritage. Without saying anything, he walked back to the bed.

Tracy felt exhausted and she knew she looked dreadful. Yet Adrian, when he returned to her side, stood looking at her as if he were regarding a miracle. After all she had been through, it helped enormously to have him look at her like that. "Isn't he beautiful?" she murmured. "He came out the wrong way."

"He is beautiful and so are you. And now you are going to go to sleep."

She nodded a little and the nurse came into the room behind them. "Thank you, my love," he said softly and, bending, kissed her on the mouth.

As he reached the bottom of the stairs on his way to rejoin the doctor in the library, he was surprised to see a large number of people assembled in the hall. It seemed as if half the servants in the house must be there the Duke thought. He smiled a little. "Her Grace has had a son," he said, telling them what he supposed they wanted to hear.

There was little change in the expressions before him. Then Wilton said, "And Her Grace is well, I hope?" The Duke suddenly realized that all these people were worried about his wife. He was surprised and deeply touched.

"Her Grace is well," he said. "Tired, but well." And the faces before him split into smiles. He thought, with wonder, as he proceeded toward the library, that he had not been the only one keeping vigil through that day.

Chapter 20

Is love a tender thing? It is too rough,
Too rude, too boist'rous, and it pricks like thorn.
                                        —Shakespeare

It took Tracy a long time to recover from childbirth. Physically, she was exhausted. She had had a
difficult delivery and she found nursing the baby
painful and draining. But she fought her fatigue, refused to admit it to either her doctor or her
husband. She had always been so splendidly healthy
that she had had no experience with physical
weakness; she tended to regard it as a moral flaw in
herself that she should be so constantly tired.

Her mental state was even more seriously
depressed than her physical one. She found herself
missing her father dreadfully. There was a great pit
of loss inside her whenever she realized that he
would never see this little grandson, would never
play with him on the floor or take him sailing off
Beachy Head.

She was homesick. Tears came to her eyes whenever she heard someone call her baby his little lord-

ship or Lord Hythe. It seemed a measure of her foreignness that she should be the only one to call her son Billy. Even Adrian called him by the more formal William.

She hid her grief and her homesickness as well as her fatigue. The outward face she presented to the world did not at all reflect her inner state. But the toll of concealment was severe; dammed up inside, all her feelings—perfectly normal feelings of postchildbirth depression and fatigue, grief for a lost parent and homesickness—created a pressure of terrible tension. Denied any outlet, they festered instead of healed.

One of the results of this inward turmoil was that she began to doubt herself. She became convinced of her own inferiority and inadequacy as a wife. The Duke had returned to his governmental duties and was once more traveling back and forth to London. Tracy felt horribly guilty that she was making him live a kind of life that involved constant travel and a part-time wife. She was an inadequate wife in other ways too. Sexually, she just could not respond to him, and after one or two times he had ceased to approach her. He was being infinitely patient, and that made her feel guilty too.

She was mired in the depths of depression and feelings of inferiority for months. Adrian knew there was something wrong; she saw him looking at her, concern and puzzlement in his eyes, but she could not speak to him of her troubles. His own traditions, she knew, were stoic; if he felt weariness or grief or fear he would deal with it privately and carry on. She could not cry on his shoulder that she missed her father and her country. She could not say that she loved her son but he tired her unendurably. She could not tell him that she felt a failure as a wife. He would be all sympathy and reassurance, she knew, but she was horribly afraid that he would secretly think her a failure.

The image of the Comtesse d'Aubigny rose to haunt her. She could never imagine that elegant woman of the world allowing herself to get into such a miserable emotional knot. She could not imagine the Comtesse ever failing, as she was failing, in the important business of social representation. The Comtesse would always be by her husband's side, would entertain for him with efficiency and brilliance, would always uphold in the social world the same high standard he himself did in the political world.

As May progressed and the beautiful English countryside was at its glorious best, Tracy became more and more convinced that she must go up to London with Adrian. He had been given a Cabinet post and was busier than ever now that the Congress of Aix La Chapelle was over and some basic decisions had been made about foreign policy. He was a very, very important personage and it was time his wife came out of hiding and assumed her appointed, her expected, her imposed, character.

Adrian had never once suggested that he wanted her to go up to London with him. She thought, somewhat hollowly, that he probably thought she was incapable of assuming the duties and responsibilities of her station. He probably thought that all she was good for was to stay at home, pickling and gardening.

She was dreadfully afraid that that *was* all she was good for. The London world was so tremendously fixed and ordered. It demanded things be done on a grand scale. All the great people of the land, such as Lady Bridgewater, would be watching her with merciless attention, waiting for her to fail. She felt sick at the very thought of having to face that world and compete in it.

But as the weeks went by she became more and more convinced that she would have to face it. She owed it to Adrian. If his wife constantly failed to do what by rights he would expect of her, then she could not complain if he looked elsewhere for what she did not give. She thought again, with hatred, of the Comtesse d'Aubigny.

Her mind was made up on a cool spring evening late in the month. The Duke had been in London for almost a week and he seemed, to Tracy, more absent than ever before. Too absent. She could not go on like this she thought as she stared into the fire. She was dressed for dinner and waiting for Mary and Miss Alden to join her. When the door opened behind her she turned, expecting to see them, and there instead was her husband.

"Adrian." She had hoped to see him earlier, but when he had not arrived she had resigned herself to another endless day's absence. He stood before her for a moment as though revealed, so perfectly beautiful and so generous in his grace that she felt again the stab of inferiority. How could she ever hope to be worthy of him?

He came across the room and held her close and long. "How are you, *ma mie?*" he murmured, scanning her face.

"Fine, now that you are here."

They spoke for perhaps three minutes, then he said, "Am I too late for dinner?"

"Certainly not. Do you want to dine right away, or do you want to change?"

"Change," he said firmly. "If you don't mind waiting?"

"Of course not." She watched him walk through the door, but, even in his absence, the room seemed filled with his presence. She would go up to London with him. She would conquer all her private demons and do for him and be to him all that he would wish for in a wife.

Mary came in and said, "I see Adrian has arrived."

Tracy smiled peacefully. "Yes." She felt better now that her decision had been made.

The Duke was not perfectly pleased with her announced intention. "Come to London with me! But you're still nursing the baby, Tracy."

"He can come with us. He is sleeping through the night now. There is no reason for me to be as tied down as I have been."

"It will be too tiring for you," he protested. "The country is quieter, less demanding. I'm afraid London will wear you out."

"Nonsense, Adrian," Tracy retorted rather sharply. She had been touched on a sore point. "I am perfectly fine." There was doubt in the Duke's dark blue eyes. "Unless, of course, you don't want me to come," she added stiffly.

"Of course I want you, *ma mie*," he said quietly.

"Good. Then that's settled." She turned to address a remark to Miss Alden.

They sat together in intimate silence after dinner and listened to Mary play the piano. The beautiful music, beautifully played, lifted Tracy out of herself. For the first time in too long she felt high above the pits of despair and inadequacy in which she had been mired. All her stumbling blocks were below her. For the first time in months she felt she would be able to do what she desired.

When Adrian took her hands in his as they stood together over their sleeping baby, she felt herself melting and going to pieces as she had not done since before Billy's birth. He put an arm about her and, held close to his side, she slowly walked with him into her bedroom.

Adrian was deeply worried about Tracy. He watched her closely, thinking, waiting, fearing. At first he had told himself that her strained look and unaccustomed silences were caused by fatigue. But as time went by and he caught her several times with tearstains on her face, he began to fear it was something more serious. He began to fear she was regretting her marriage.

For the Duke his wife had come to be, quite simply, the most important thing in life. He had loved many other women, but his interest had always waned with his possession. With his wife the reverse was true. The more she surrendered to him, the more her power over him increased. It had become the focal point of his life: to know she was there, was his, was his wife. It shook him to the very core of his being, the fear that she was with-drawing from him, the fear that he was losing her.

He had only one way of expressing himself to a woman, but Tracy did not want him to make love to her. With a restraint he had not known he possessed, he contained himself and did not ask her for what she could not freely give. And, through-out all the long days and nights of the long months, he remained faithful to her.

It was not because he was not tempted. London was filled with beautiful, willing women and the months of abstinence were very long. He was tempted. But he was, for all his enlightenment, a man of strange superstitions. He had always be-lieved in his luck, but he had always felt he deserved his luck. He stayed faithful to Tracy mainly due to this obscure superstition. If he be-trayed her—his dearest love, his golden girl—he was putting all of his happiness into jeopardy.

And it seemed that his patience was finally bear-ing fruit. Her responsiveness to him on the night of his return had been like a manna in the desert. As they drove together up to London, he hoped that all their trouble was now over. He hoped, fer-vently, that he had got his wife back again.

Chapter 21

Thy looks with me, thy heart in other place.
                              —Shakespeare

The American political situation was once again about to create a disturbance in the lives of the Duke and Duchess of Hastings. The uproar over General Jackson's executions of Ambrister and Arbuthnot had quite blown over, the two victims being written off by the British government as a necessary debit in the balance sheet of Anglo-American affairs. Spain, realizing that it could not count on aid from Britain, had finally gotten on with negotiations over the Floridas, and on February 22 the Spanish Ambassador to the United States and Secretary of State John Quincy Adams had signed Adams' masterpiece, the Transcontinental Treaty. For the first time, the boundaries of the United States stretched from ocean to ocean. Two days later the Senate of the United States had unanimously advised and consented to the treaty's ratification.

The Duke and the Duchess entered into the affair at the point where the treaty was sent to Spain to be ratified by the King. The United States sent a new Minister to Madrid to accomplish this task. He was John Forsyth of Georgia, a likable, intelligent man who had no previous diplomatic experience and who was further handicapped by the fact that he spoke no language but English. In the corrupt, misty atmosphere of the Spanish Court, he was like a bull who has blundered into a nest of mosquitoes. The King refused to ratify the treaty, saying it ceded too much land, and John Forsyth did not know what to do. In his confusion, he blamed the King's intransigence on the British, convincing himself that the British government was ready to support Ferdinand in his annulment of the treaty in return for the cession of Cuba.

In order to allay the American's suspicions, Lord Castlereagh offered to send to Spain the Duke of Hastings, who spoke fluent Spanish and who had well-known American ties.

The Duke was not pleased when news of this assignment greeted his return to London with Tracy. He did not want to leave her at just this moment when relations between them were happier than they had been in months, but his sense of duty would not allow him to refuse the mission. Very possibly he would have refused, however, if he had realized that the ship's captain who had brought John Forsyth from America to Spain was crossing from Spain to England at the very moment the Duke was planning to embark in the opposite direction. Adam Lancaster, of Salem, Massachusetts, was coming to see the girl he had once hoped very much to marry.

＊　　＊　　＊

Tracy was not as disturbed about the Duke's proposed trip as he was. Once she had decided to undertake her public role as Adrian's wife, she had sworn to herself that she would make a success of it. After a great deal of hard thought, she decided to go to Lady Bridgewater and ask for assistance. Adrian's aunt had heretofore figured in her mind rather as a serpent in the garden of her private paradise, but she remembered something her father had once said about the advisability of turning enemies into friends. It sounded like a good idea. If she could convert Lady Bridgewater from critic to ally, her battle would be half won.

Lady Bridgewater was delighted when Tracy approached her for advice. She was by nature a managing woman and the prospect of managing the young Duchess was irresistible. It was not that she had ever precisely disapproved of Tracy; it was simply that she was solicitous for her nephew's position. In fact, Tracy had been in her good graces before she had returned to London. Lady Bridgewater had heard the news of Mr. Bodmin's death with discreet satisfaction. It was so nice to know that all those millions would come rolling into the ducal coffers. And then Tracy had so promptly presented her husband with a son and heir. So when the Duchess turned up at Lady Bridgewater's door, pretty and bright as a new gold guinea, anxious to assume her social duties and eager to be taught the proper way to carry them out, Lady Bridgewater was all gracious encouragement.

The Duke's aunt thought Tracy should plan a

ball for July. "It isn't really that onerous a task, my dear," she said to Tracy kindly. "And I will assist you."

Actually, the plunge back into London society was very good for Tracy. The open admiration of so many great men was a great boost to her self-esteem. For the first time in months she began to feel that she was pretty. Her old electric vitality returned. Mary had come to London with them and the two girls shopped for clothes and drove in the park in the brilliant sunshine. Rather to her own surprise Tracy found she was enjoying herself.

One reason was that she had finally physically recovered from her postnatal fatigue and depression. And a great deal of the uneasiness that had plagued her previous London season had been dispelled. She knew her husband better. She no longer worried that he would take to gambling; Mary's revelations about his confrontations with his father on that failing had put to rest all her doubts on that score. Nor did she fear that he would be unfaithful to her, not, at least, if she gave him no cause. She was the mother of his son. And she thought that he cared for her, a little. She would bind him to her with hoops of steel. She would be a brilliant hostess for him. She would give him an army of children. After two weeks in London, encouraged by Lady Bridgewater and by the admiration of her glittering circle, she felt she could do it all.

Adrian's departure for Spain came at a rather convenient time for Tracy. She was finding her feet and was determined to give the biggest, brightest, most successful ball of the whole Season. She was going to work like a laborer over it, but she did not want him to see how important it was to her. Adrian would expect his wife to be able to organize balls merely by waving a wand, she felt. It was just as well that he was going to be out of her way for a while.

So the face Tracy showed her husband on his departure was more cheerful than it had been for some time. Unfortunately, Adrian would have been happier if she had been less so. It seemed to him that she was glad to get rid of him.

He had a very trying time in Spain, which was not helped by his misgivings about Tracy. First of all, he had to sail from Southampton down through the Bay of Biscay to Santander and traveling by water always made him sick. Secondly, the situation in Madrid was enough to drive any rational man insane.

He tried first to convince some members of the Spanish Council of State that according to international law an absolute monarch was bound to ratify a treaty signed by a minister with full powers. But the Council of State, smarting from some extremely honest remarks by the American Minister, advised the King not to ratify the treaty. International law be damned, they felt.

The Duke then devoted himself to holding the hand of the American Minister. Mr. Forsyth wanted to go home. "This is a situation I find personally irksome and one in which, furthermore, I am useless to the United States," he told the Duke. "I do not have the experience to handle this matter successfully."

"Do not blame yourself, Mr. Forsyth," the Duke soothed him. "A more experienced man than yourself would be driven to despair by trying to make sense of this Court. No diplomat, however brilliant, can divine a policy where no policy exists." The Duke also managed to convince Mr. Forsyth that the British government was not opposed to the Transcontinental Treaty.

The Duke wrote privately to Lord Castlereagh. "The Spanish government wants the United States to agree not to recognize the revolutionary governments in South America. They won't ratify the treaty unless they get a guarantee of that. There is nothing more Britain can do in the matter at present." Then, after doing what he could to bolster the American Minister's spirits and having demonstrated to Spain and to the rest of Europe that the British government supported the Transcontinental Treaty and did not want to annex Cuba, the Duke took ship for home. He was extremely anxious to see his wife once again.

Chapter 22

He of tall building and of goodly pride.
                                        —Shakespeare

The Duke was not the only one who was anxious
to see Tracy. He would have been profoundly disturbed if he had known that one of the ships he
had passed on his uncomfortable journey to Spain
carried the "friend" from Salem whose letter had
so ruffled him in December.

Adam Lancaster had been dealt a severe blow by
the news that Tracy was to marry the Duke of
Hastings. The only thing that had prevented him
from setting sail immediately for England was the
realization that he would be too late. By the time
he arrived, she would be married.

As time went on he had not become reconciled
to losing her. He could not get her out of his mind.
Next to Tracy's shining memory, every other girl
he met seemed dull and lifeless.

He had had little doubt that William Bodmin was
the architect of Tracy's marriage. When Mr. Bodmin had returned to Salem, Adam had gone to see

him, fire flashing in his hot brown eyes. But Tracy's father had suddenly become a very sick man and Adam left unsaid all of the things he had planned to say. Mr. Bodmin had been so clearly delighted by his daughter's marriage. And then there had come another piece of news, news Adam had found as painful as her father had found it happy. Tracy was expecting a child.

Adam had tried to put her from his mind. He bought several ships from William Bodmin and threw himself into his business. Salem was declining in importance as a port and Adam was looking seriously into the possibility of moving to New York.

Adam Lancaster was twenty-nine years of age. Though he had started his career as a cabin boy, he was now a millionaire. During the late war with England he had commanded the *Massachusetts*, the most successful privateering ship out of Salem. He had accounted for twenty-six British ships and had been a considerable embarrassment to the Royal Navy. His prizes of war had sold for over a million dollars, and his fortune had been rising ever since.

He had been too busy to think of marriage. Until, that is, he met Teresa Bodmin. She had just come home from school and he had seen her in church on Sunday morning. He had called to see Mr. Bodmin that afternoon and gotten himself formally introduced. He had called frequently after that, and it soon became understood in Salem that Tracy Bodmin and Adam Lancaster would make a match of it.

Adam had thought that Tracy would marry him. He had wanted to make the engagement formal before she left for England, but she had put him off.

Nevertheless, he had had little doubt that when she returned home, they would marry.

It had not happened that way. Tracy had been coerced by her father into marrying a decadent English aristocrat—to Adam's mind all aristocrats were decadent—and she had been irrevocably divided from him. However, as day succeeded day and her memory did not fade, Adam began to wonder how Tracy's marriage was faring. He thought he would pay a visit to England and see for himself.

When Adam Lancaster arrived in London, he went first to see Richard Rush, who graciously insisted that Adam stay with him. From Rush he learned what he could about Tracy. To Adam's dismay, the American Minister appeared to be an admirer of the Duke of Hastings.

"He is in Madrid at the moment," Rush told Adam as they had a glass of Madeira together. "Forsyth was in a rare taking and Lord Castlereagh asked the Duke to see what he could do to unravel the snarl over the ratification of the treaty. If it can be unsnarled at all, he is the man to do it."

Adam gave a cynical bark of laughter. "I doubt if it can be," he said briefly. "I never saw a sorrier collection of scoundrels in my life than the idiots that run the Spanish government. Poor Forsyth. He hasn't the stomach to deal with them. No American would have."

The emphasis was slight, but Rush found himself moving to the Duke's defense. "Hastings is a highly honorable man, I assure you, but he has the subtlety of mind one usually finds in Europeans rather than Americans. He will understand better how to deal with rascals."

Adam's lip curled slightly, but he refrained from answering. Clearly this husband of Tracy's was a serpent, he thought as he rose to his impressive height. "Tracy and I are old friends from Salem," he said instead. "I think I'll go round to see her now that I'm here."

Richard Rush surveyed the splendid masculine figure in front of him; it was not difficult to believe that Adam Lancaster had amassed a fortune before the age of thirty. "If I might make a suggestion?" Rush said hesitantly.

"Well? What is it, man?"

"Your clothes, Captain Lancaster."

Adam looked astonished. "My clothes? What about them?"

"They won't do for London. They won't do for the Duchess." Adam began to glower and Rush continued hastily, "I don't mean to suggest that Her Grace would not be pleased to receive an old friend, no matter what his attire, but if you are to be here for a while she will doubtless want to introduce you about. You owe it to her to make a creditable appearance, Captain Lancaster. You owe it," concluded Richard Rush rather grandly, "to your country."

Adam's sense of humor got the better of him. "Oh," he said gravely, "if it is a matter of my *country*."

Richard Rush grinned a little sheepishly. "Well, they do place an inordinate amount of emphasis on the proper clothing over here."

"Hah!" snorted Adam. "They would." Richard

Rush looked a little unhappy; he genuinely liked the English. "Don't worry, Rush," Adam said, misreading his expression. "I won't disgrace you. Where do I have to go to get rigged out?"

The figure who presented himself at Hastings House two days later looked the very model of an English gentleman. From his well-cut blue coat to his fawn pantaloons and gleaming Hessians, he was a perfect advertisement for Weston's excellent tailoring. The only startling thing about him was his unusually large size.

The door was opened by a frosty-looking butler, who took Adam's name and said he would see whether Her Grace was at home. He then showed Adam into an extremely elegant anteroom and disappeared, closing the door behind him. Adam paced about, finding his heart was beating uncomfortably fast, and strained his ears for the sound of steps. They came and almost instantly the door opened.

"Adam!" Tracy said, surprise, pleasure and a hint of wariness in her voice. "What brings you to London? How lovely to see you." She crossed the room to give him her hand. He took it and held it and for a minute they both remembered vividly the more intimate gesture of their last meeting. Tracy took her hand back from his strong grasp, her color heightened.

"You look wonderful, Trace," he said, his deep voice unmistakably sincere.

"And so do you!" She stepped back and regarded him with admiration. "Weston," she said.

He grinned. "Rush told me I owed it to my

country to buy myself some new clothes. I wouldn't have minded so much if my old ones had been even a *little* worn."

Tracy chuckled appreciatively. "What a lovely New England attitude, Adam. I hope you saved them?"

"Of course I did!" He looked so surprised that her chuckle turned to a laugh.

"Come along with me to the morning parlor," she said. "It's more comfortable than this room and we can have some tea and a nice long chat." She put her fingers lightly on his arm to guide him, and it seemed to him that he could feel her touch right through Mr. Weston's elegant blue superfine coat. He glanced down at her brown-blonde head as she walked him along, talking gaily. He had forgotten how beautiful her hair was, he thought as he replied automatically to a question. He had thought he remembered her smile, but memory had not done it justice. He followed her into a larger room that looked as elegant to his eyes as the one they had just left—and just as as uncomfortable. The butler came into the room after them.

"Do you desire any refreshment, Your Grace?"

"Oh, yes, Wilton, thank you. Tea, please. And some cakes, perhaps."

"Yes, Your Grace." The man left and Tracy turned to find Adam staring at her in perturbation.

"Is that what they call you over here? 'Your Grace?'"

Tracy's eyes danced. "Yes."

"*Everybody?*"

Tracy leaned forward, serious now. "You wouldn't believe it, Adam. There are probably only eight people in the whole of England who call me Tracy. They just *love* titles over here. I think they positively enjoy your-gracing and my-lording people to death. I still haven't gotten used to it."

This was very promising news and Adam felt himself relaxing a little. "I understand from Rush that your husband is in Spain," he said cautiously.

"Yes, he went over to try to rescue Mr. Forsyth. Isn't it funny? You must have crossed each other somewhere along the way."

"I guess so," said Adam. "He is quite a diplomat, then, the Duke?"

"There is no one who is more diplomatic than Adrian," Tracy said positively. "Lord Castlereagh utterly relies on him. If anyone can sort the Spanish out, Adrian will." Adam, to whom diplomacy was a synonym for duplicity, looked pleased.

The tea came, brought by another manservant whom Tracy called Robert. Tracy poured Adam a cup and said in a constricted voice, "Did you see much of Papa, Adam, before he died?"

"Yes," he said gently.

"How—how was he?"

Adam told her. "He was a very brave man, Trace," he concluded. "I hope, when it's my turn to go, I can do it with as much grace."

Tracy had been staring steadily out the window during his recital, but now she turned to him. "Thank you, Adam. I needed to know. I felt so helpless over here, so cut off. Wondering every day if he were in pain, if he wanted me . . ."

"But you didn't know," Adam said in bewilderment.

"Yes," she said simply, her mouth set in an unaccustomedly severe line. "I knew. It was his wish that I didn't and so I went along with the pretense. But I knew."

"I see," said Adam very slowly. It seemed to him a blinding light had just been shed on the reason for Tracy's marriage. "When someone you love is dying, naturally you would do anything he wanted."

"Naturally," said Tracy in return.

Chapter 23

Thou dost love her, because thou know'st
   I love her.

                  —Shakespeare

Tracy found that she was indeed very glad to see Adam Lancaster. The initial embarrassment she had felt at their first meeting quickly disappeared; and since he made no attempt to bring up their previous relationship, she soon felt very comfortable with him.

It was so good to hear her own language again! Richard Rush was the only other American she saw with any frequency, and he was becoming more British with every passing day. Adam was New England. He was Salem—natural, real, with American humor, American understanding, American openness. Tracy found his company both comforting and exhilarating.

She was proud to introduce him to her new friends and relatives. He was so manly, so strong and good looking, that he was bound to make a good impression. And he did. The Duchess' American friend, Captain Lancaster, enjoyed a popularity among the *ton* that would have surprised a more knowledgeable socialite than himself. Part of the good will extended to him was a desire to please Tracy; it had become very clear to those in the know that the new Duchess of Hastings was going to *count* seriously in London society. And part of Adam's welcome was due to himself; the ladies found him fascinating.

Tracy was extremely busy planning her ball, which was set for July 18. Adrian had fully expected to be home at least a week earlier than the date she had chosen and so she went forward with her plans in his absence. Lady Bridgewater was proving to be invaluable. She and Tracy spent one or two hours together every day during which time the Countess answered Tracy's many questions and discoursed in detail about the minutiae of the great London world.

Tracy confided to Adam her nervousness over the coming affair. "It will be the first party I have thrown, Adam, and it must be right. No. It must be more than right. It must be *memorable*."

"Really, Trace," he said with a frown, "a party can't be all that important."

"It is," she insisted tensely. "It is important for Adrian that his wife do things properly, that she do them with style. He has a very high position in this country, you see, and they all set great store by things like entertaining properly."

Adam's brown eyes looked at her with an unreadable expression in their darkness. "It's very different from Salem," he said noncommittally.

"It certainly is," she replied fervently. "A summer party in Salem would be a fishing expedition on the bay followed by a marvelous chowder cooked in an iron pot on Baker's island." She closed her eyes. "Chowder," she said reverently.

"I'd like to see Lady Bridgewater's face if you offered to sail her to an island to eat chowder," Adam said dryly and Tracy giggled.

It was a wet summer evening in July and Adam Lancaster, Richard Rush and Lord and Lady Bridgewater had all come to Hastings House for a dinner that Tracy described as a family party. She had allowed Mary to join them and had been pleased by Adam's attentiveness to her young sister-in-law. They all retired to the drawing room after dinner and Tracy encouraged Adam to talk about some of his experiences in Russia. Lord Bridgewater was a very influential man, and Tracy didn't think it would hurt Adam at all to become better acquainted with him.

William Bodmin had made tremendous profits trading with Russia before the War of 1812 and Adam had sailed one of his ships. "Most shipmasters wintered in Riga," Adam was saying. "It was much more convivial. Only once did I make the trip around Norway to Archangel. Wintering in Archangel was an experience. The sun never once came up. It made New England seem like the tropics."

"Good heavens," said Lady Bridgewater. "Whatever did you do, Captain Lancaster?"

"What all the Russians do, my lady," replied Adam with a grin. "I drank."

They were all laughing at his reply when the door opened and the Duke stood on the threshold.

"Adrian!" cried Tracy, turning her laughing face toward him. She jumped up and crossed the room. "You're home at last!"

He kissed her cheek. "Home at last," he murmured.

"And about time," said his aunt. "There is a ball planned for which you are to be the host, if you remember."

He smiled at Lady Bridgewater tranquilly. "I remember. I said I would be home in time and I am." He then greeted the rest of the assembled guests, was introduced to Adam Lancaster and accepted a cup of tea from his wife.

Richard Rush began to question him about Spain and Tracy sat down behind the tea tray again, her eyes attentive to her husband's face. After some minutes she noticed that he had finished his tea and, rising, she went and relieved him of his cup. He shook his head to say he did not want another and she put it down on the chimney piece and stayed for a minute behind his chair, her hand on its polished wood back.

He and Adam were talking about Spain, but Tracy only half heard what they were saying. When Adam turned to say something to Richard Rush, Tracy gently rubbed her forefinger along the back of Adrian's neck. His lids came half down to veil his eyes, and he smiled without looking at her. After a minute she returned to her seat.

Adam was being bitterly scornful about the Spanish King, whose iniquities he had observed firsthand. The Duke listened courteously and, without saying so, managed to imply he thought such a diatribe was in bad taste. Tracy smiled a little as she listened to him. She knew very well that in his heart of hearts Adrian agreed with every word Adam had said about Ferdinand. But this was not the company in which he would ever reveal such feelings. She must, Tracy thought vaguely, remember to explain that to Adam.

After what seemed to Tracy an interminable time, her guests bestirred themselves to leave. Mary had gone to bed earlier and the Duke and Duchess themselves accompanied their departing guests to the front hall. As the door closed behind them, the Duke turned to his wife, his veiling lids lifted so she could clearly see what was in his eyes. "And now, *ma mie*," he said softly, "I can attend to you."

Tracy awoke late the next morning and sighed with contentment as her eyes rested on Adrian, asleep next to her in the bed. She felt languorous and lazy and full of love. Luxuriously, she stretched a little and turned as she heard a soft chuckle. "You look like a cat," he said.

"Mmnn. I think I feel rather like a cat. A nice, fat, sensuous, satisfied cat."

His hand slid lightly across her flat stomach and slim flank. "Hardly fat," he murmured.

They had made passionate love the night before. It had been many months since Tracy had felt such excitement, such total abandonment. She had thought she was replete, but at his touch, and to her surprise, her body awoke.

Adrian felt the tremor deep within her abdomen. "Ah," he said. "How nice."

"I have to nurse Billy," she protested rather feebly.

"Billy can wait," her husband said firmly.

She felt herself open and aching for him. "Adrian," she whispered. Then she was filled with him, her body brimming, flooding, as she clung to him, arching her back. They kissed. Slowly, they toppled sideways, still locked together, their hearts racing, their bodies damp with a light sheen of sweat.

"I missed you," she said after a while.

"It is almost worth going away if this is the reception I can expect to come home to."

She chuckled. "You don't have to go away."

"I am very glad to hear that, *ma mie*. The next trip I make, I'll take you with me."

"That's a good idea," she approved. "Once the baby is weaned . . ." She pulled away from him and abruptly sat up. "Good heavens, the baby. He's probably starving."

"It won't hurt him to wait for a bit," said his loving father, pulling her back down. "I was hungrier."

Chapter 24

... all bitterness and wretchedness that young
men feel, in a manner continually, as jealousies,
suspicions, disdeigns, angers, desperations, and
certain rages full of madness, whereby many
times they be led into so great error ...
—*The Book of the Courtier*

Adam Lancaster had been surprised by the Duke.
He had expected Tracy's husband to be much
older. A duke, he had vaguely thought, must be
somewhere around forty. This Duke, he discovered
by inquiring of Richard Rush, was twenty-seven—
two years younger than himself. And even Adam
could not fail to notice that Adrian was extraordinarily good looking. Adam began to fear that
Tracy's marriage was not what he had thought it
to be. He needed more information, and with characteristic thoroughness, he set about getting it. It
was not difficult. London, it seemed, was full of
people who loved to gossip.

He had married her for her money. That was
what became clear to Adam as he listened to people

respond to his careful inquiries. As Americans, he and Tracy were outsiders in the magic English world of birth and position. Tracy had been acceptable because of her father's money. Money was the only reason a personage like the Duke of Hastings would have stooped to marry the daughter of an American businessman.

He had married her for her money. And she had married him because her dying father had wished it. The Duke had probably known about William Bodmin's illness, Adam thought viciously. It wasn't just a matter of a marriage settlement; with Tracy came all the millions intact.

Tracy was obviously uncomfortable in her new situation; she felt inferior. That thought made Adam wild. Tracy Bodmin, to his mind, was worth every damn duchess and countess in the whole goddamn island, and to see her worry about throwing a party for people who weren't worthy to lick her shoes put him into a rage. It was her husband. He was obviously after her to behave as he wished, to play her proper role as an English duchess. Adam found himself disliking, even more than he had previously, the princely young man who was the Duke of Hastings.

Tracy herself spoke very little of her husband to Adam. Considering the fact that Adam had once desired to marry her himself, she thought it would be tactless to dwell upon her present marital happiness. Consequently, and without her realizing it, Adrian figured primarily in her conversation as someone whom she had to live up to.

It was the way she felt. She felt that she didn't deserve him, that she wasn't the wife he ought to

THE AMERICAN DUCHESS   197

have. He was the fastest rising star in the British government, yet except in a few rare instances, he couldn't discuss his work with his wife. He was married to a woman who disagreed with almost everything he believed in. He was one of the highest personages in a very high and ancient society, and he was married to a woman who didn't even know how to throw a party properly.

Tracy did not feel inferior in herself, but she did feel inadequate as the wife of a Duke of Hastings. She was striving so hard to win her place in the world because she felt she owed it to him. She owed it to him because she adored him and to her mind nothing was good enough for him. That, however, was not the impression she gave Adam Lancaster. To Adam it seemed rather as if Tracy regarded her husband as an ogre.

Adam was not the only person to be misled by Tracy's behavior. The Duke, too, was laboring under a growing misapprehension about the nature of his wife's regard for Adam Lancaster.

The change in Tracy from the last months was blindingly clear. At first the Duke had thought that she had finally recovered from childbirth and so had regained her old vividness and sparkle. Her welcome home to him had been deeply gratifying. But as the days went by, he began to wonder if the change in Tracy wasn't due instead to the presence of Adam Lancaster.

He was certain that Lancaster was the "friend" whose letter had so discomposed Tracy in December. During the week that preceded Tracy's ball, Adrian became more and more convinced that Lancaster had been more than a friend to his wife. He did not like the American at all. He did not like it that he was so damn rugged looking and tall. He did not like the way he called his wife Trace. He did not like the easy intimacy that reigned between the two Americans. He was terribly afraid that Tracy might once have loved this man. He was even more afraid that she might love him still.

He had to know. He was having tea with her on the afternoon before the day set for their ball when he determined to bring the subject up. He sipped his tea, regarded her over the rim of his cup and asked gently, "How well did you know Captain Lancaster in America, Tracy?"

She blushed and his fingers tightened on the saucer. "He lived in Salem, Adrian, and he was one of my father's captains before he became an owner himself."

"You mean you grew up knowing him?"

"Well, not exactly. I was away at school a great deal, you see." His silence indicated clearly that he did _not_ see and Tracy bit her lip. "I really only met Adam after I left school and came home to live." She looked at her husband and smiled a little ruefully. "I suppose there's no harm in telling you. I almost married Adam, Adrian."

He put his teacup down, rose and walked restlessly to the chimney piece. "Almost?" he asked.

"Yes. Adam wanted to become engaged before Papa and I left for England, but I said I wanted to wait until we returned before I made any decision." She shrugged gracefully. "You know what happened next."

He stood near the chimney piece, his fingers

lightly laced together, looking hard at the tea table, not at her. "Yes," he said quietly. "I know what happened next."

"I was a little embarrassed when Adam first arrived in England," she confessed. "I felt guilty, I suppose. But he has been splendid."

"Yes. You seem to be enjoying his company."

"I am. I was feeling a little homesick, I'm afraid. It's been like a breath of New England to see Adam. He's of *my* race, you see. We speak the same language, have the same traditions; we see the world through the same lenses, are held together by the same moral paste."

Adrian did not like what he was hearing. "Your race?" he protested lightly. "Surely, *ma mie*, you and I are of the same race, at least."

She put down her own cup and looked for a minute in silence at her husband's face. "No," she said then, very softly. "We're not."

Tracy's revelation about her past relationship with Adam Lancaster only exacerbated Adrian's fears. It was not that he suspected her of having an affair with Lancaster. He had far too much regard for Tracy's honesty for that. Whatever Tracy did, it would be done out in the open; she was a creature of the sun, not of the shadows. What he feared was far more complicated. He was afraid that she had loved this Lancaster and that she had given him up to please her father. He was afraid that, even though she would be loyal to her marriage, she loved the American still. And it was not enough for Adrian that his wife would be faithful to her marriage. He wanted much more from her than that.

To put it bluntly, for the first time in his life, Adrian was jealous. And he was helpless in that jealously. There was nothing he could do, nothing he could accuse her of. She was responsive and passionate in bed. He knew he would sound ridiculous complaining about any lack of affection from her. But, also for the first time, he doubted the emotional truthfulness of sex. He was a superb lover. He knew that. It was the ultimate magic he had always employed in his relationships with women, in his relationship with his wife. *He knew how* to employ it. But now, it seemed unsatisfactory to him. He wanted more. He wanted the satisfaction of knowing that his wife loved him totally, completely, utterly—him alone, no one else. He wanted what he had thought he had. There was a growing hatred in him for Adam Lancaster.

Meanwhile, the cause of all this misapprehension was thinking about one thing: her ball. She had sent out three hundred invitations and almost six hundred people were coming. The musicians were hired, the food was arranged for, her dress was ready. She had decided to deck the rooms with fresh flowers, and she and Lady Bridgewater had paid visits to half the flower shops in London.

The servants had been busy all week, polishing furniture and silver and washing crystal. Tracy herself spent the entire day of the ball arranging the flowers. Adrian, returning in the late afternoon, had been greeted by the sight of two huge vases of pink and red roses placed in the large entrance hall.

Following the sound of activity, he proceeded through the house to the ballroom in the center of which, slowly revolving to regard her handiwork, he found his wife.

The room looked beautiful. The polished floor gleamed. The crystal chandelier sparkled. And arranged throughout the room were stunning masses of pink and red roses. "A masterpiece," he said and she turned at the sound of his voice.

"Do you like it, Adrian?"

He walked into the room. "Yes, very much." He smiled at her. "Roses. You would think of roses, *ma mie*."

"You don't think it's too much?"

"I think it is perfect."

She smiled. "I like it too." She slipped her hand through his arm. "We have people coming for dinner first, remember. It must be almost time to change."

"Yes, I suppose so. What are you wearing, Tracy? You've been very quiet about this whole affair, you know."

Adrian was the only person in her immediate circle to whom she *had* been reticent on the subject of this ball. She didn't want him to know how much trouble she had taken and how worried she had been. "You'll see," she said now, a mischievous gleam in her eyes. "It's a surprise."

Chapter 25

For love, thou know'st, is full of jealousy.
                                            —Shakespeare

Tracy's ball was one of the last of the Season and, by common consent of the *ton*, the most brilliant. The dinner party that preceded it was attended by, among others, Lord and Lady Castlereagh; the Prince and Princesse de Lieven; the Prince and Princess Esterhazy; the Earl and Countess of Bridgewater; the Duke of Wellington; the American Minister, Mr. Richard Rush; Captain Adam Lancaster; and a vast, glittering array of London's "best people" filled Tracy's rooms during the course of the evening. It was a triumph. The hostess herself was one of the most brilliant stars in a very brilliant galaxy.

Tracy wore the Hastings rubies, a fabulous collection of jewels that included a huge necklace, a ruby and diamond tiara and several enormous bracelets. When Adrian had given them to her, he had said ruefully, "They're worth a fortune, but you couldn't possibly want to wear them. They're

dreadfully heavy and old-fashioned, I'm afraid."
She had locked them away carefully, but when she
had thought of this ball, she had thought once
more of the rubies.

Adrian's face, when he saw her, told her she had
been right. Her deeply décolleté, white satin dress
was fitted closely to her waist and fell in graceful
fullness to the floor. It was not fashionable, but on
Tracy's tall, narrow-waisted figure, it was exquisite.
And it was the perfect style to show off the rubies.
The rubies were Tracy's costume, not the dress.

They glowed against her skin—rich, warm, in-
describably beautiful. The necklace, on her, did not
look at all heavy. It might have been made just to
adorn that long, slender neck, to rest on just those
full, young breasts. As she surveyed herself before
leaving her room, Tracy remarked to Emma, "I
never could have worn this dress, or carried off
this great expanse of rubies, before Billy."

Both girls laughed at her words and Emma said
sincerely, "I think, Your Grace, you could carry
off anything."

It seemed the *ton* agreed with her. The amazing
thing was that the rubies, stunning as they were,
did not eclipse the wearer. Tracy's smile was as
brilliant as her jewels. She combined magnificence
and friendliness. Her party might be a ball for six
hundred people, but Tracy, bred in American hos-
pitality, felt she must speak to as many of her guests
as she possibly could. Very few people left without
having had the gratification of a few words with
the Duchess.

The Duke was not so gregarious, but he did not
need to be. People always knew where he was, in

the way they always did, and his princely transcendence was an immensely gratifying thing in itself. He was not a man who needed to *do* anything to establish his preeminence. He simply had to be.

Tracy was thinking something like this as she watched her husband in conversation with the Prince Regent. As she watched Adrian turn his generous grace on the monumentally fat, carefully primped figure of his sovereign, there was no doubt at all in Tracy's mind who was the more royal of the two. And Adrian *worked*, she thought vehemently to herself. He had all the gifts of fortune and leisure, yet he worked. She might not agree with everything he did, but she admired his dedication tremendously. And she really couldn't see how he could bring himself to be so sublimely deferential to the Prince Regent.

"He must spend three quarters of the day eating," said a cynical voice in her ear. She turned to regard Adam Lancaster. "How on earth do you bring yourself to curtsey to him?" he asked in unconscious echo of her own thoughts.

"It was really difficult the first time I had to do it," she confessed. "But he is so ridiculous, Adam, that one finds one can't take the whole thing seriously."

"Your husband must take him seriously," he said.

She shrugged a little. "Adrian's loyalty is as impeccable as his manners. He will never say what he thinks, and certainly not to such die-hard republicans as ourselves." This was not strictly true. Tracy knew what Adrian thought about the Prince Regent, but *her* loyalty kept her from telling

Adam. "Are you enjoying yourself?" she asked him with a smile.

"Very much. But I would like to dance with you."

"I don't have time to dance, Adam. I'm the hostess."

"You can dance once at least." She looked longingly toward the floor. Tracy loved to dance.

"Oh, all right," she said, laying her hand on his arm. "I do deserve at least one break from my labors!" The two Americans moved onto the floor together and as they made a very handsome couple, they attracted more than a few pairs of eyes. One of those pairs belonged to the Duke.

After the last guest had departed, Tracy turned to her husband as they stood together in the hall and said, "I'm exhausted. It's much more fun to go to a ball than it is to give one."

"I know what you mean. I didn't realize there were as many dowagers in the whole of London as the number who descended on us tonight."

Tracy looked at him curiously. "Were you actually talking to dowagers, Adrian?"

"I was not. They were talking to me."

She laughed. "I think it was a success," she said with a note of inquiry.

"Assuredly it was a success. You have established yourself as a brilliant hostess, *ma mie*. And if you are even half as tired as I am, I think you ought to come to bed."

Tracy was conscious of a flash of annoyance. She didn't consider Adrian was being appreciative enough of her triumph. She wanted to be praised and lauded and all he did was say he was tired and wanted to go to bed. Of course, since she had never confided any of her anxieties to him, he was unaware of her present sense of jubilation and victory. She had striven to present him with the appearance of one to whom giving balls was as easy and unimportant as carding wool, but now that he failed to exult with her in her success, she was irritated. It crossed her mind that she was being unfair, but the irritation persisted.

"You go on upstairs," she said to him, her voice unaccustomedly clipped. "I am going to the kitchen to tell the servants to go to bed and not to stir until nine tomorrow. They have all worked like horses." And off she marched, her back straight as a lance, a general on her way to dismiss the troops. Adrian watched her go, a shadow deepening the dark blue of his eyes.

All these misinterpretations of Tracy's feelings came to a head the following evening. Tracy had had a very lazy day, recuperating from her exertions of the night before. She and Mary went for a drive in the park in the late afternoon and then had dinner alone together, as Adrian had left word he would be dining with Lord Castlereagh at White's. The sisters-in-law discussed with pleasure the prospect of returning to Steyning Castle in a few days. They both were looking forward to seeing Lord Harry, who had been at the Castle for most of the month. London had held little appeal for fifteen-year-old Harry and his visits to Hastings House had been brief. He was better off, Tracy realized, in the country with his horses.

After dinner both Tracy and Mary went upstairs to play with the baby and put him to bed, then Mary went off to her room to write and Tracy settled down in the library with *Rob Roy*. She had been reading for perhaps an hour when Wilton came in to announce that Captain Lancaster had called and wished to see her. Tracy was surprised but told Wilton to show him into the library.

"Adam!" Her surprise was faintly audible in her voice. "What brings you here this evening? Adrian is not home, I'm afraid."

"I know," said Adam. "I saw him earlier at White's."

"Oh," she said rather blankly.

"Tracy"—he came across the room and took her hands in his large, hard grasp—"I've got to talk to you."

She tried to pull her hands away, but he held them more tightly. "What about?" she said, bewilderment mingling with alarm.

"I've been trying to say this to you for days now. It seems I never get a chance to be alone with you. I want you to come back to America with me."

"What?"

"I love you," he said intensely. "I have always loved you. Come away with me. You aren't happy here. You know you aren't. You only married him because of your father."

"No." She was staring up at him in distress. "Or, yes, I did, but things have changed . . ."

"My feelings haven't changed," he said passionately. "Come with me, Tracy. He'll get a divorce and then we can marry. Let him keep the money. It's what he wants, and we don't need it. I have plenty and I'll make more."

She was looking up at him, her eyes wide with alarm, her lips slightly parted, ready to protest. "I love you," he muttered and, pulling her hard against him, bent his head and kissed her. For a moment Tracy was still, her senses reeling with the shock of his words, of his totally unexpected embrace. Then indignation finally overcame surprise, and she raised her hands to push him away.

From the doorway came her husband's voice. "May I ask what is going on here?"

Adam released her and she whirled away from him, turning to see Adrian in the doorway. The look she saw on his face caused her throat to dry and her heart to start pounding.

"I'm glad you came home," Adam said. "I want to talk to you."

"Tracy," said the Duke, "go upstairs, please."

"Adrian . . ." she breathed, pleadingly. She had never been so frightened in her life. She looked at the two men in the room with her—Adam so huge and dark and grim, Adrian so slender, so icily composed—and knew that her husband was the more dangerous. "Adrian, please," she said.

"Go upstairs." He spoke quietly without heat, but she knew that he was very angry indeed. He didn't look at her as she passed next to him and once she was in the hall, he closed the door behind her. She was trembling all over as she climbed the stairs to her room.

Chapter 26

Thy love is better than high birth to me,
Richer than wealth, prouder than garment's cost,
Of more delight than hawks or horses be.
                                        —Shakespeare

The next few hours were the longest Tracy had
ever spent in her life. She dismissed Emma and
paced about for a while, then she went next door
to look at her sleeping baby. She moved about the
room, deliberately making noise, and when he
woke and cried she picked him up and held him
close to her, rocking and comforting him, trying to
comfort herself with his sweet warmth. She sat
down and nursed him for a little and then, when he
fell back to sleep with her nipple still in his mouth,
she sat holding him for ten more minutes before
she gently put him back into his crib.

There was still no sign of movement in Adrian's
room, so Tracy slowly undressed herself and got
into bed. She did not lay down but sat, propped
against her pillows, her dilated eyes fixed on the
door that led to her husband's room. After what

seemed a very long time, she heard footsteps next door, and then the sound of voices. A door closed and footsteps sounded in the hallway. He had dismissed his valet, Tracy thought. The night was warm, but she was shivering as she stared at the unmoving door. At last it opened and Adrian was there. He came into her room and stood silently, looking at her as she sat upright in the huge bed. Her shining hair was tumbling in curls over her slender shoulders. She wore a thin green nightgown and her arms and shoulders were bare. Her eyes in the glow of the lamp were huge. She looked very frightened.

He was still fully dressed, his neckcloth immaculately tied, his black coat buttoned. The fact that he had not undressed for bed frightened Tracy even more. He was not going to make love to her. The thought flashed through her mind, leaving profound dismay in its wake. "Adrian . . ." she said again, her voice a thread of sound in the silent room.

"I understand from Lancaster that you wish to leave me." She couldn't speak; she only continued to stare at him out of enormous green eyes. "He was kind enough to inform me that I might keep your father's money. Evidently you neglected to tell him about the trust fund." He spoke with a bitterness that astonished her.

After a moment she managed to push words out of her constricted throat. "I don't want to leave you."

"*Oh?* I am very glad to hear that, *ma mie*, because I've no intention of letting you go." His face was pale and set. She had never seen him look so stern.

"What did you do to Adam?" The words were barely a whisper.

He looked at her in silence for a minute and when he finally spoke his voice was even. "Nothing. I came very close to killing him. Very close." His mouth twisted a little. "But, of course, it would have made such a scandal. And I do not want a scandal."

"There won't be a duel?"

"There won't be a duel." He turned away from her to look out of the window at the dark garden. "Your reputation would never survive a duel, Tracy," he said. "Captain Lancaster is safe."

It took a moment for his words to register, but when they did, the terror that had gripped her began to subside. "I don't care about Adam Lancaster!" she cried, feeling the blood begin to flow through her veins again. The worst had not happened. Adrian was not going to send her away and he was not going to shoot Adam. She knelt up in the bed, able once more to speak and urgent now to reach him. "Adrian, you must listen to me. What happened tonight—it was not my fault! Adam came in and all of a sudden he was asking me to go to America with him and I was so stunned I didn't know what to say and then he started kissing me. It all happened so quickly! I don't know what got into him, but truly truly I did not encourage him. He had only been with me five minutes before you came in! You can ask Wilton if you don't believe me."

He listened to her in silence, his back still to her as he stared out the window. He listened. And he did believe her. What he could not forget, however, were Adam Lancaster's words, "She only married you to please her father. She loved me, but she married you because her father was dying." That was what the Duke believed too.

"Adrian . . ." Her voice was trembling. She was on the brink of tears. He turned to her, a little wearily, a little impatiently.

"Yes," he said. "I believe you."

She looked at his beautiful, reserved face and the tears began to slide down her cheeks. "I'm sorry," she whispered. "I am such a bad wife, but I do love you so. I don't know why Adam did what he did tonight. I thought he had forgotten all that, as I have."

"What did you say?" His voice held a note she had never heard before.

The tears came even faster and she tried to wipe them away with her wrist as she answered. "I said I know I am the wrong wife for you. You deserve someone who is regal and dignified and who knows how to entertain and how to be a duchess. I try, but I never learned those things, and I know I'm not the right wife for a man like you. You can't even discuss your work with me, because half of it I don't understand and the other half I don't agree with." She gave up trying to wipe away her tears and let them fall unregarded as she lifted her face to look at him. "But I love you," she said. "You could search this earth over and you'd never find anyone who could love you more."

He came across the small space that separated him from the bed. "Is that the kind of wife you think I want?" he asked harshly, "the kind of person you have just said you are not?"

Her tears had stopped and lay now sparkling on her upturned face. "Don't you?" she asked faintly.

"No!" His voice was unusually loud, almost violent. "I do not want a wife like this bloodless paragon you have just described. I do not want to come home and talk politics to my wife when I have been talking nothing but politics all day long to endless rows of ambassadors and government ministers. I want to come home to someone who is alive and vital and who has seen and done and spoken about things that are *not* politics. I want to hear a voice that is different from the voices I hear all day, and half the night too, at receptions and balls. I want to come home to you. I want to be married to you. What do you think it means to me to know I have you"—his eyes swept over her face, her thinly veiled breasts, her bare arms and shoulders—"waiting for me, sharing my life, my bed, mothering my son? Do you really think I would have let you go, even had you wanted to?"

Tracy had never seen his emotions so nakedly revealed, never heard him speak in such a voice. Her heart had begun to hammer once again, but not in fear this time. She stared at his face, and what she saw there caused a great tide of joy to begin to well up within her. "I thought you loved Lancaster," he was saying, and his voice had still not returned to its normal cadence. "All this last week, I have felt like murder. If this were the sixteenth and not the nineteenth century, I would have put a bullet into all six feet three inches of him."

Strangely, Tracy's democratic instincts were not at all outraged by this very feudal statement. In fact, the glow within her spread to her face, which now looked illuminated from within. Even the tears on her cheeks seemed radiant. "I didn't know," she said, "I didn't know you loved me like that."

His eyes were darker than midnight. "How did you think I loved you?"

She shook her head a little. "I don't know. I guess I thought you were fond of me and would be loyal to me, but I never thought you loved me half as much as I loved you."

"You wouldn't have married me if your father hadn't wanted you to."

"No." She got off the bed and went to stand before him, putting her arms around his waist, resting her cheek against his shoulder. "You fascinated me," she said softly. "You were unlike anyone I had ever met. But I would not have married you." She pulled back a little and tipped her head to look at him. "But by the time we returned from our honeymoon, I thought that the greatest bliss life could offer me was to be your wife. I wanted to live to worship you, to die to serve you. Surely you know that? Adrian? Surely you know that your touch is sweeter than heaven to me, your presence all that makes my life worthwhile."

He was staring down at her with a look that suddenly recalled to her his expression when he had looked at her after Billy was born. "Tracy," he said only. "Tracy." He pulled her against him, holding her so tightly that she could scarcely breathe. She didn't complain, however, but locked her own arms around him and pressed her cheek into his shoulder. They remained that way for a long, silent minute. Finally she moved, and his hold on her relaxed a little. She put her hands up to his neckcloth. "You forgot to get undressed," she said.

His eyes smiled down at her. "So I did."

Her fingers were busy at his throat and he raised his hands to cover them. "Let me do it," he said. "You'll take too long."

It did not take the Duke long at all and this time their lovemaking, which had always been passionate, swept them both into a blinding, shattering rapture that was beyond what either had ever experienced before. It was a very long time before they had any inclination toward rational conversation.

"I think you had better go see Lancaster tomorrow," he said much much later.

She yawned a little as she stretched herself alongside him. Finally, lying still now, "Why?"

"I don't want to see him and he certainly won't want to see me. One of us, however, has obviously got to pack him off home."

"I guess so," she murmured, her mind clearly not on Adam. Then, "Today, not tomorrow. It must be morning by now."

"Mmn."

Softly she asked, "Did you mind what he said about the money?"

His fingers, which had been caressing her scalp through her hair, stilled. "Yes."

"Don't. It doesn't matter. I married you at Papa's wish and you married me because of Papa's money. Neither motive is important now. Why we married doesn't count." His fingers began to move again on her head and she said slowly, "That was why you made Papa set up the trust fund, wasn't it?"

"Yes. I did not want you to think . . ." His voice trailed off.

"Well, I don't," she said tranquilly and yawned again.

"You're not tired?" he said reproachfully.

"I'm exhausted!"

His mouth came closer to hers. "Are you sure of that?" he asked softly. Her lips were warm and yielding under his and he raised his head a little to look down at her, a faint smile in his eyes. "Are you quite, quite sure?"

It seemed, after all, that she was not.

About the Author

Joan Wolf is a native of New York City who presently resides in Milford, Connecticut, with her husband and two young children. She taught high school English in New York for nine years and took up writing when she retired to rear a family. Her previous books—THE COUNTER-FEIT MARRIAGE, A KIND OR HONOR, A LONDON SEASON, A DIFFICULT TRUCE, THE SCOTTISH LORD, and HIS LORD-SHIP'S MISTRESS—are also available in Signet editions.

More Regency Romances from SIGNET